"You'd know if you'd ever had a crush," said Cassie. "You'd feel all tingly and shaky and you get little shivers in your stomach. Sometimes you feel dizzy, too. That's when you really know."

"Sounds like the flu," Lydia replied, and set off for school, practically giddy with excitement. It was a bit like the feeling Cassie had described, but as far as Lydia was concerned, this had to be better. Who needed boys and dates and crushes when you had a great cause to get involved with?

Titles by Marilyn Kaye available in Lions

THE SISTERS SERIES

Phoebe
Daphne
Cassie
Lydia

THE THREE OF A KIND SERIES

1. With Friends Like These, Who Needs Enemies?
2. Home's a Nice Place to Visit,
   But I Wouldn't Want to Live There
3. Will the Real Becka Morgan Please Stand Up?

Marilyn Kaye

Lydia

Lions

An Imprint of HarperCollins*Publishers*

First published in the USA 1987 by
Harcourt Brace Jovanovich, Publishers
First published in Great Britain 1988 in Lions
This impression 1991

Lions is an imprint of
HarperCollins Children's Books,
part of HarperCollins Publishers Ltd,
77–85 Fulham Palace Road
Hammersmith, London W6 8JB

Printed and bound in Great Britain by
HarperCollins Manufacturing, Glasgow

For Ilene Cooper

1

LYDIA GRAY STORMED INTO the kitchen, threw her books on the counter, and made a general announcement to the group gathered around the table.

"George Philips is a moron. He's an idiot. He's the biggest jerk, the biggest nerd, the biggest—"

"Whoa!" her father interrupted. "Enough! I think we get the picture."

"You're late again, Lydia," Mrs. Gray said. "Sit down and eat."

Lydia yanked out a chair and plunked herself down. "I don't know how any ninth-grade human being can be so incredibly stupid," she muttered. "They should send him back to elementary school."

No one responded. Her parents and her three sisters

calmly continued passing bowls and platters and filling their plates. They'd all heard this before.

At least Daphne had the courtesy to look concerned. She brushed her dark bangs out of her eyes, pushed her glasses up from where they'd slid down her nose, and offered Lydia a sympathetic smile. "What did George do this time?"

Lydia raised her eyes to the heavens, as if she was searching for strength. With a look of grim fury, she stabbed her fork into the platter of meat.

"Good grief, Lydia," her mother said mildly, "that's just roast beef. It's not George lying there."

"Wish it was," Lydia growled. "How that toad got to be editor of the *Cedar Century* is beyond me."

Cassie threw her one-year-older sister a look of barely concealed scorn. "He got to be editor because everyone knew you'd turn the school paper into . . . I don't know, into something weird. They figured you'd use it to start a revolution."

"That's ridiculous," Lydia replied.

"Face it," Cassie continued complacently, "your ideas are just too crazy for junior high."

Phoebe, the youngest sister, looked up indignantly. "Lydia's ideas aren't crazy." She paused, and then added, "At least, most of them aren't."

Cassie gave her a withering glance. "How would you know? You're not even *in* junior high."

"So what?" was Phoebe's rapid-fire response.

"Girls," Mrs. Gray said automatically. "Lydia, why don't you calm down and tell us what happened."

For a moment, Lydia chewed in angry silence and swallowed. "I want the paper to deal with important news, major social issues. George wants dippy garbage."

"Can you be a little more specific?" Mr. Gray asked.

Lydia sighed heavily. "He wanted a piece on cheerleaders. So I gave him this terrific editorial on cheerleading uniforms. And today he told me it's not what he had in mind and he won't even run it!"

"Cheerleading uniforms," her father mused. "I didn't know that was a major social issue at Cedar Park Junior High."

Lydia nodded. "They're disgusting. It absolutely amazes me that any self-respecting female would wear something like that in public."

"I think they're cute," Cassie commented.

"Cute?! They're sexist! Have you noticed the way the boys stare at those girls? Half the time they're not even watching the game. They're just waiting for the girls to do one of their leaps so they can see their pants."

"They're *supposed* to see the pants," Cassie said. "That's why they match the skirts."

Lydia ignored her. "And they're not very practical. On cold days you can actually see the cheerleaders' legs turning blue."

"How come George turned down your article?" Phoebe asked.

"He said it was boring. He wants something like 'A Day in the Life of a Cheerleader'—you know, something glamorous. He doesn't think anyone's interested in hearing about how sexist the uniforms are."

3

"Maybe he's right," Daphne offered tentatively. "I mean, I've never heard anyone talking about it at school."

Lydia turned to her father. "But shouldn't a newspaper educate people about what's important? And not just give them what they want?"

Mr. Gray looked thoughtful. "I'd say a newspaper has to do both. As an editor, I try to write editorials that raise issues and give some perspective on them. But that doesn't mean we can't have advice columns and horoscopes and recipes."

"And comics," Phoebe offered helpfully.

"That's right," Mr. Gray said. "And society news, Hollywood gossip, that sort of thing."

Lydia nodded regretfully. "George is starting a gossip column. You know, like 'What class officer has been seen hanging around the Burger Monster with what certain track star?' Dumb stuff like that."

"Cassie, you're not eating," Mrs. Gray said.

Cassie had frozen, poised with a forkful of string beans halfway to her mouth. Her eyes were glazed. " 'What class officer . . .' " she repeated, her brow furrowed. "Did he say which class?"

Lydia rolled her eyes in despair.

"What do the other kids on the staff think of George?" Mr. Gray asked.

Lydia shrugged. "Most of them just go along with everything he says. Kevin thinks he's a jerk, though. And so does Martha Jane. She wanted to do a feature story on health and fitness. And he said okay, but only if she has some girl in a sexy leotard pose for photos.

I'm telling you, the guy makes me sick. He's ruined the paper. Working on it is no fun at all anymore."

"If it's so awful, why don't you just drop out?" Phoebe asked.

"I've been thinking about it," Lydia admitted. "But I can't imagine not working on a newspaper anymore."

"You could work on the literary magazine," Daphne suggested. "We always need more people."

"I guess I could," Lydia said, but her voice carried little in the way of enthusiasm. That literary stuff, poems and all, was fine for Daphne. But it didn't much appeal to Lydia. How could she get into writing about flowers and birds and rainbows when there was a world out there that needed changing? Okay, maybe she couldn't change the world—but surely she could make a few changes at Cedar Park Junior High.

"If I dropped off the staff, it would be like giving in to George," she said. "I keep telling myself that if I stay on, I'm bound to have *some* impact."

"That's the spirit," her mother said encouragingly.

Lydia managed a thin smile. "But most of the time I feel like I'm banging my head against a brick wall."

"You do get some of your articles in," Daphne reminded her. "Like that one last week about the need for rest room improvement."

Lydia brightened slightly. "That was pretty good, huh? But the only reason it got in was because George was out sick the day we went to press. I substituted it for the joke column." She giggled. "I thought George was going to kill me."

"*I* wanted to kill you," Cassie said. "Writing about

bathrooms! It was so embarrassing. Especially the part about the boys' rest room. Totally gross. Did you really go inside? What if someone had been in there?"

Lydia grinned. "Kevin guarded the door for me. It was pretty interesting." She started describing what she'd seen, but her mother interrupted.

"Lydia, not while we're eating, okay?"

"Huh?" Lydia looked at her blankly. "Oh. Okay, Mom. Anyway, I'm glad it got published, but I hated having to sneak it in like that. Dad, you're so lucky to be editor of your very own newspaper. You can do anything you want."

Mr. Gray laughed. "Hardly! I have a publisher to answer to, you know. And I was just a lowly reporter once, too. I've had to deal with my share of editors I didn't get along with."

Mrs. Gray smiled at him. "I remember when you were just starting out, in Chicago. The names you called that poor man! You were worse than Lydia."

"Well, I was just out of college, Lois, remember. And I was used to running my own show."

Lydia looked at him with interest. "Were you editor of your college newspaper?"

"Not the official paper," her father said. "This was the late sixties, and there was a lot of disagreement on campus as to what sort of position the college paper should take."

"The college newspaper was pretty conservative," Mrs. Gray said. "So your father and some of his friends started their own newspaper."

"We called it the *Campus Alternative*," Mr. Gray added.

6

"What kinds of things did you write about?" Lydia asked.

"Oh, the issues of the day," her father said. "The war in Vietnam, civil rights . . . there was so much going on in the world, and I didn't want to waste my time reporting on fraternity parties."

"There were campus issues, too," her mother continued. "For example, in the dormitories, women had curfews and men didn't."

"How come?" Phoebe asked.

Daphne explained. "That was in the olden days, when people thought girls were inferior to boys."

"It wasn't *that* long ago," Mrs. Gray said pointedly. "Anyway, that's how your father and I met." Her eyes became cloudy with reminiscence. "He was covering a campus demonstration. The women were protesting dormitory regulations. I was president of my dorm, and your father interviewed me."

"So you see, Lydia," Mr. Gray said, "we're not exactly unsympathetic to your problems. We understand how you're feeling. The question is, what are you going to do about the situation?"

Lydia didn't reply. She was staring into space, looking like she'd gone into a trance.

"Lydia?"

Lydia blinked. "That's it!" she exclaimed. "That's it!" Everyone stared at her.

"What's it?" Phoebe asked.

Lydia jumped up. "Can I be excused for a minute?" Without waiting for a reply, she ran out of the room and upstairs to the telephone alcove in the hall. Quickly, she dialed a number, tapping her foot impatiently while it rang.

"Martha Jane? Hi, it's Lydia. Listen, I have the most fabulous idea for the paper. Can you meet me tomorrow at school?"

"Sure, I guess so. In the *Century* office?"

"No! Uh, let's meet in the cafeteria, at lunch."

"What's this all about?"

"I'll tell you tomorrow. And look, isn't Kevin in your homeroom? Tell him to meet with us, too."

"Gee, you're sounding so mysterious. Do you want me to tell anyone else to come?"

"I don't know. . . . Can you think of anyone else who can't stand George Philips?"

"Oh, wow!" Martha Jane squealed. "Are we going to start up a revolt and get him fired?"

"No, nothing like that. Just bring anyone you know who thinks the *Cedar Century* stinks."

"Maybe Emma Reese," Martha Jane said. "Lydia, can't you just give me a hint what this is all about?"

Lydia debated. She could tell Martha Jane right then and there . . . but she thought her idea might have more impact if she explained it in person.

"Lydia, you haven't finished your dinner," came her mother's voice from downstairs.

"I have to go," Lydia said in a rush. "I'll see you tomorrow." She hung up the phone and ran back downstairs.

"What's going on?" her mother asked.

Lydia sat down and beamed at them. "How does this

sound?" She paused dramatically, and then leaned forward. "The *Cedar Park Junior High Alternative.*"

Her sisters just stared at her, with expressions ranging from interested to puzzled. But her father let out a deep, prolonged sigh of resignation, and turned to her mother.

"Me and my big mouth."

2

THE ROUTINE CHAOS of the school cafeteria at lunchtime was in full swing. Lydia was oblivious to it. Her full attention was focused on the faces of her three table companions.

"Are you serious? Start our own newspaper?" Martha Jane's eyebrows shot up above the rims of her oversized glasses.

"And we'll call it the *Cedar Park Junior High Alternative*. Or maybe just the *Alternative*." Lydia leaned back in her chair. "Well, what do you guys think?"

She didn't really need to ask. Their expressions said it all. Martha Jane's mouth was still open. Emma Reese looked stunned, as if she'd just been hit in the face with a pie. A grin slowly spread across Kevin's freckled face, and his eyes were gleaming.

"Our very own newspaper," Martha Jane said thoughtfully. "Could we do it?"

"Why not?" Lydia replied. "My father did it when he was in college. He got sick of working on his boring school paper, so he and some friends quit and started their own."

"But where are we going to get the money for it?" Emma asked. The dazed look had disappeared from her face and now she only looked dubious.

Lydia stared at her while she tried to formulate an answer. She didn't know Emma very well, and she didn't want the pretty, soft-spoken girl to know she hadn't even thought about that.

"Emma's got a point," Kevin said, his grin fading. "Newspapers cost money. And you know the school's not going to pay for two newspapers."

Martha Jane agreed. "Especially since the *Alternative* will be publishing articles that might not make the administration happy."

Lydia liked the way Martha Jane said "will be," as if the *Alternative* was already a fact. She thought rapidly. "Maybe it doesn't have to cost very much. It doesn't have to look like a newspaper. After all, it's the content that counts."

Kevin nodded. "That's true. We could just type it up and copy it."

"But even that costs money," Emma objected. "And I don't have any."

Lydia frowned at her. This girl was being very negative, and Lydia was beginning to have doubts about bringing her into the plan.

11

"Maybe not so much money," Kevin said. "I've got a cousin who owns a photocopy store. I'll bet he'd give us a good deal."

"And we'd only need to come up with money for the first issue," Lydia reminded them. "If we sell the paper for ten cents a copy, we'll have the money we need to put out the next issue."

"We're going to *sell* it?" Emma looked quizzical. "Do you think kids will actually pay for a newspaper?"

"Sure," Kevin said. "As long as it's just a dime. And if we keep the size of the paper down to two or three pages, I'll bet my cousin will run it off for ten cents an issue. We won't make a profit, but we'll break even."

"That's assuming we sell all of them," Emma reminded him.

Lydia frowned at her again. Emma Reese did not have the right attitude. She decided to get them off the boring topic of money and onto the exciting stuff. "Think of the possibilities! We can write about anything we want, all those issues that George is too chicken to touch."

Martha Jane seemed to appreciate that. "I'm so sick of covering those stupid Pep Club meetings. Who cares whether they have red sweatshirts with white letters or white sweatshirts with red letters?"

"We won't have to waste our time on junk like that," Lydia replied. "We're going to deal with *real* issues."

"Like what?" Kevin asked.

Lydia opened her mouth to tell him, and then quickly clamped it shut. George Philips was approaching them.

The short, chunky boy lumbered over to their table.

He greeted them in his usual pompous way, and then fixed a stern eye on Lydia. "Have you finished rewriting that cheerleading article?"

Lydia turned to him smugly. "No, I haven't. And I'm not going to." She paused for effect. "I'm resigning from the *Century* staff, George."

George blinked. "You are?"

"We all are," Lydia added. "Aren't we?" She looked at the others. They all responded with varying degrees of agreement—Kevin bobbing his head fervently, Martha Jane with a little apologetic smile, Emma with a small nod.

"We're starting our own newspaper," Lydia told him. "You better watch out, George! You're going to have some real competition." She tried to make that sound fairly friendly. After all, she didn't want to upset George *too* much.

George didn't look upset at all. He gazed down at Lydia condescendingly. "Now, Lydia," he said, in a way that sounded like a parent talking to a fussy child, "be realistic. This school doesn't need two newspapers."

"Oh, yes it does," Lydia responded spiritedly. "We need a paper that's going to raise some issues! A paper that's not afraid to take a stand!"

George appeared mildly offended. "The *Century* takes stands! What about the Pep Club controversy? The *Century* is definitely supporting red letters on white sweatshirts."

Martha Jane sniffed. "That's hardly what I'd call controversial, George."

"We're going to take positions on serious concerns,"

Lydia stated firmly. "Even if they're unpopular positions. Even if they go against school policy."

George raised his eyebrows. "You could get into trouble, you know."

Lydia recalled hearing that line in a TV show. Happily, she also remembered the actor's response. " 'Trouble,' " she recited solemnly, " 'is my middle name.' "

George just stared at her. Then his familiar expression returned. "Well, good luck." His words carried a patronizing tone that infuriated her, but he walked away before she could think of a good comeback.

Emma was looking at her uneasily. "What kind of trouble?"

"Huh?"

"George said we could get into trouble."

Lydia dismissed that with a wave of her hand. But Kevin was looking a little disturbed, too.

"You know, Mr. Fletcher isn't going to be thrilled if we start criticizing school policy."

Lydia had to admit he was probably right. Their principal was always giving upbeat assembly speeches about school spirit, teamwork, and looking on the bright side. She had a feeling he wouldn't appreciate criticism—even the constructive kind.

"I don't want to get into trouble," Emma murmured.

Lydia faced her squarely. "We can't get into trouble. There's freedom of the press in this country, remember?"

"I know we have freedom of the press in this country," Emma said. "But the question is, do we have freedom of the press in this school?"

Lydia wasn't sure, but she replied with as much conviction as she could muster. "Absolutely."

She looked at the others. Kevin seemed pensive. Martha Jane was biting her lower lip. Were they having second thoughts? Lydia leaned forward.

"We have to take some risks with this paper! We have to meet challenges head-on! And as long as we don't break any rules, we can't get into any real trouble. C'mon, you guys. We have an opportunity here to make some real changes at this school. This is our last year at Cedar Park Junior High. We owe it to the seventh and eighth graders to make this a better place! Let's leave them with something to remember us by!"

She stopped and took a deep breath. It was a good speech. And it seemed to be having an effect.

"You're right," Kevin said. "Let's do it." His eyes were gleaming again. Martha Jane was smiling brightly, and even Emma seemed to have caught a spark of enthusiasm.

"Okay," Lydia said happily. She pulled a notebook and pen out of her backpack. "Let's talk about the first issue. What's going to be in it?"

"How about that article on cheerleading uniforms that George turned down?" Martha Jane suggested.

Lydia shook her head. "Not for the first issue. We need something bigger, something that will grab everyone's attention. If the newspaper's going to be only a couple of pages, we'll probably be able to deal with just one problem a week. The first issue should deal with something everyone's interested in, something dramatic and startling."

"How about abolishing cheerleading altogether?" Kevin asked.

"That's not bad." Lydia opened the notebook and wrote *Ideas* in big letters on the top of a page. Under that, she wrote *1. Abolish cheerleading*.

"You know what I don't like?" Emma said suddenly. "The honor code."

Everyone turned to her in surprise. "Emma!" Martha Jane exclaimed. "Do you . . . do you cheat?"

Emma's face flushed. "Of course not. But have you ever actually read that code they make us sign? It doesn't just say you promise not to cheat. It says you have to turn in anyone you see cheating. And I don't think it's right to make us promise to be tattletales."

"I never thought about that," Kevin mused. "I mean, what if you saw your best friend cheating?"

"Good point," Lydia said, writing down *2. Abolish honor code*. "What else?"

"Phys ed," Kevin said. "I don't think it should be required. The kids who are naturally athletic get A's and the rest of us get B's, no matter how hard we try."

"You're right," Martha Jane said. "Of course, I always get A's in phys ed." She preened a little. "But then, I'm a natural athlete. On the other hand, what if they required us to take piano? I'd be flunking out of school."

Lydia laughed. Martha Jane had been forced to take piano for three years—and she still had problems pounding out the scales. But her logic was right on target.

"It's not fair," she agreed. "Athletic ability is like

singing or dancing or any other kind of talent. You either have it or you don't. So we shouldn't be graded on it." To her list, she added *3. Abolish phys ed requirement.*

"And what about the Junior Princess contest?" Martha Jane continued. "It's so sexist. We should abolish that."

This was getting really exciting. There were so many things to choose from, so much to attack!

"Okay," Lydia said. "Now let's think of which subject to hit in the first issue. It should be the one we think most kids will get really worked up about." She turned her notebook around so they could all study the list.

Everyone fell silent as they pondered the various topics. Junior Princess, honor code. . . . Lost in thought, Lydia's eyes drifted to a couple of boys talking at the table next to them.

One of them poked his fork into his food and made a face. "This stuff's disgusting. How do they expect us to eat this garbage?"

"No kidding," the other boy said. "It'll probably stunt our growth."

Lydia looked down at her own barely touched tray. She'd had the same thought for almost three years. Just a few weeks ago, she'd been planning a petition to do something about the cafeteria food. But then she'd gotten caught up in other things. . . .

The food was disgusting. And like a seed growing silently in the back of her mind, then suddenly bursting into bloom, a notion became a full-fledged idea. "I've got it!" she cried out. "The one issue I'll bet every kid in this school agrees on!"

17

"What?" the others asked in unison.

"Cafeteria food! It stinks! And we could make that our first official cause."

Their reaction wasn't very satisfying. Kevin just looked skeptical. "That's old stuff, Lydia. It's *ordinary*. Every student at this school has been complaining about the food since day one."

"Exactly," Lydia declared. "Everyone complains about it. But nobody *does* anything about it. We won't just be complaining. We're going to take action!"

"Actually, that's a pretty good idea," Emma remarked. "It's something everyone cares about."

Martha Jane bobbed her head vigorously. "And it would get a lot of kids to support the newspaper if we start off with campaigning for better food."

"Maybe," Kevin said cautiously. "*If* we could come up with a new approach to the campaign . . ."

"And that's exactly what we'll do!" Lydia announced happily. She glanced at the clock. It was almost time for class. "Tomorrow's Saturday. Let's everyone meet at my house at three."

They all agreed. "But we have to come up with an original way to deal with this," Kevin warned as he got up and lifted his tray from the table. He glanced down at what was left of its contents and made a face. "You know, I don't even know what it was I just ate."

"And it probably wasn't even good for us," Emma added, rising.

Lydia grinned at her. Maybe Emma would be okay after all.

"It's a great idea," Martha Jane said. "The newspaper *and* the campaign. I'll see you later, Lydia."

Lydia knew she should get up and take off if she was going to make it to class on time. But she wanted to sit there for a moment and savor her good feelings. There was nothing she liked better than getting a project started. And this one promised to be a biggie.

Her thoughts were interrupted when Cassie came dashing up, her face flushed and her blonde hair flying.

"What are you doing here?" Lydia asked. "I thought you had an early lunch period."

"I just ran in between classes. I was looking for you."

"What's up?"

Cassie sat down at the table across from her and leaned over. "Do you know Zack Snyder?"

"Sure. He's on Student Council. Why?"

Cassie didn't answer that. "How well do you know him?"

"Not very. Why are you so interested in Zack Snyder?"

"Because he's adorable!" Cassie swooned. "And he *winked* at me when I was coming out of the gym this morning."

Lydia groaned. "Zack Snyder winks at anyone who's remotely female, Cassie. He thinks he's the number one hunk of the universe."

"He *is*," Cassie giggled. "Find out if he's got a girl-friend, okay?"

"What happened to what's-his-name? Gary Stein?"

Cassie shrugged. "Oh, Gary's still around. But he's only an eighth grader."

"So what? *You're* only an eighth grader."

Now it was Cassie's turn to look exasperated. "But there's a ninth-grade dance in two weeks. And maybe I could get Zack to invite me."

Lydia shook her head wearily and stood up. "I have to get to class—and so do you."

"Okay," Cassie said. "But just see if you can find out if he's involved with someone. I don't want to waste my time flirting with him if he's already got a date."

Lydia sighed in resignation as she watched her sister's retreating figure. Boys, boys, boys. That's all Cassie ever thought about.

Thank goodness *she* had more important things on *her* mind.

3

LYDIA SURVEYED the living room scene with dismay. Her father was sprawled on the couch, his eyes glued to the football game on TV. On the floor, Phoebe and her friend Linn sat surrounded by magazines and scraps of cutout pages.

"Can you guys clear out?" she asked. "Some kids are coming over and we need space to work."

"Can't," Phoebe replied succinctly. "We're working on a class project."

"Where's Mom?" Maybe *she* could clear them out.

"Out shopping with Daphne," Phoebe said. "Linn, pass me the scissors."

Lydia turned to her father. "Dad, we're going to be working on the newspaper. Do you *have* to watch that game?"

"Yep." Her father's eyes didn't leave the screen. "Work in your bedroom."

"We can't," Lydia said. "It's a mess. Besides, Cassie's in there."

"No, I'm not," Cassie said, entering the room. "I'm going out and you can have the room all to yourself."

"Where are you going?" Mr. Gray asked.

Cassie paused to examine herself in the mirror over the fireplace. "Over to school, to watch the football team practice."

Mr. Gray actually turned his head slightly to give her a look of mild surprise. "Since when are you so interested in football?"

"Since I found out Zack Snyder is cocaptain of the team," Cassie replied, making a minor and unnecessary adjustment to her hair. "I'm meeting Barbie, and we're going to pretend we're just out for a walk."

Lydia rolled her eyes as Cassie grabbed her jacket and ran out the door. But Phoebe's friend Linn was looking after her with unconcealed admiration. "Wow, she really knows how to go after a boy."

"Yeah, she's very talented," Lydia said sarcastically. "Dad, we still can't work in the bedroom. Cassie's side is a mess." Realistically, she had to admit her own side wasn't that much neater. But at least her part of the room was covered with books and papers. Cassie had probably left underwear lying on her floor.

Reluctantly, Mr. Gray turned away from the television again. "Forgive me if I'm mistaken," he said, "but I seem to recall that we have a kitchen with a table."

"Okay, okay, I guess we can work in there."

"Excellent idea," her father murmured, returning to his game.

Lydia went to check out the condition of the kitchen. Luckily, someone had cleared away the remnants of lunch. She ran back up to her room to collect paper, pencils, a dictionary, and a thesaurus, then returned to distribute them around the kitchen table.

Emma arrived first. Lydia greeted her at the front door and led her through the living room. "That's my youngest sister, Fee, and her friend Linn. This is my father."

"Pleased to meet you," Emma said, glancing at the television. "What's the score?"

"Bears, 6-3," Mr. Gray said.

Lydia hurried her back to the kitchen. "Do you like football?"

Emma laughed. "Not really. But I like football players."

Lydia closed her eyes in pain. "Oh, no. Not you, too."

Emma looked at her blankly, but before she could pursue the discussion, there was a knock on the back door.

"Come on in," Lydia said to Martha Jane and Kevin. "I've got everything all set up."

"Wow, this looks really professional," Martha Jane said, eyeing the neatly arranged table with appreciation.

"I talked to my cousin," Kevin told them as they all sat down, "and he said if we can keep the first issue down to one legal-size sheet, both sides, he'll run off a hundred copies for free!"

"That's nice," Emma said, "but there're almost four hundred students in the school."

"So they'll have to share," Kevin said.

"Okay, it's better than nothing," Lydia said. "Now, I think we should start off with an introduction to the newspaper. You know, sort of a statement of purpose, what the *Alternative* is going to be."

"Like a philosophy," Martha Jane added. "Lydia, I think you should write that. After all, it's your idea."

Lydia had hoped someone would suggest that. "I've already made a few notes," she admitted. "Listen to this." She read from a paper. " 'What's wrong with Cedar Park Junior High? If you don't know now, you'll find out here. Cedar Park Junior has a lot of problems, and we're going to tell you exactly what they are.' "

"Whew," Kevin whistled, "sounds heavy."

"We have to come on strong in the first issue to get their attention," Lydia explained.

"Maybe that's a little too strong," Emma ventured.

But Lydia pretended not to hear her. "Then we could have an editorial on how bad the food is," she continued. "We should write that together. How should it start?"

"Make it simple and to the point," Kevin said. "Something like, 'The food in the cafeteria is terrible.' "

Lydia jotted that down.

"And it's not good for us, either," Martha Jane offered, and Lydia kept writing.

Emma's forehead puckered. "We don't know that for a fact. I think we have to stick to the facts."

Lydia considered. "But even if it's nutritious, if we can't eat it, it can't do us any good."

"That's logical," Martha Jane agreed. "What's next?"

"I guess we should go into detail," Lydia said. "Talk about specific things they give us to eat."

Kevin pretended to gag. "Like that junk everyone calls 'mystery meat.' "

Lydia noted that. Then she frowned. "This isn't enough. We're not going to be able to fill both sides of a legal-size paper."

"How about quoting other students?" Emma asked. "Getting a bunch of opinions and statements about the food?"

"That's a good idea," Lydia said, writing down the suggestion.

"Wait a minute," Kevin said. "We know what they're going to say, and they're all going to say the same thing: 'Food stinks,' 'It's garbage,' 'I hate it.' "

"So what?" Martha Jane asked.

Kevin grimaced. "It's going to get boring. And the last thing we want the *Alternative* to be is boring."

He was right, Lydia thought. Both sides of a page covered with complaints about food would be pretty monotonous. "But what else can we say about the food, except for how bad it is?"

No one responded. They were all silent for a moment, and then Emma spoke for all of them. "I don't know." They stared at each other helplessly. When Mr. Gray strolled into the kitchen, their eyes automatically turned to him.

He seemed taken aback by the attention. "Halftime," he announced, as if offering an explanation for his presence.

"Dad, look at this," Lydia said, handing him her notes. "We're doing our first issue on the subject of cafeteria food. Only we don't know what to say except that it stinks."

As her father took the paper and began to read, Phoebe and Linn wandered in.

"Anything to eat in here?" Phoebe asked.

Mr. Gray looked up from his reading. "Here? In the kitchen? Gee, I don't know. I once heard of someone finding food in a kitchen, but—"

"Dad!" Lydia broke in. "C'mon, we need help!"

Her father handed the notes back to her. "Well, it's a pretty negative approach."

Kevin grinned. "It's pretty negative food."

"What are you guys doing?" Phoebe asked, pulling a bag of cookies out of a cupboard.

"We're working on our newspaper," Martha Jane explained. "It's called the *Alternative*."

"Oh, yeah?" Phoebe said. "What does 'alternative' mean, anyway?"

Emma picked up the dictionary and flipped through it. " '*Alternative*. Adjective. Available in place of something else. Noun. One of two or more possibilities.' "

"There you are," Mr. Gray said. "If you're going to call this paper the *Alternative*, you need to live up to your newspaper's title. All you're doing here is attacking the food. You're not offering any alternative."

"You mean, give an example of how they could improve the food?" Lydia asked.

"That's a possibility."

"I know," Phoebe's friend Linn said. "Why don't you

26

suggest they close the cafeteria down and let everyone go to Burger Monster for lunch?"

Lydia and her friends exchanged condescending glances.

"Right," Martha Jane said kindly. "We'll take that into consideration."

"Dad, I think the game's starting up," Phoebe called from the doorway.

Mr. Gray saluted the group around the table. "Keep on truckin'," he said, walking out.

"Keep on what?" Kevin asked.

"Who knows?" Lydia picked up her pencil and started doodling in the margin. "Okay, I think maybe we should give examples of better food they could serve."

"How about shrimp?" Martha Jane suggested.

"Or lamb chops?" Kevin licked his lips.

"I don't think so," Lydia said doubtfully. "They're pretty expensive. We'd better suggest foods that cost about the same as the stuff they're giving us now."

"Comparable in cost," Emma murmured, and they all wrote that down.

"But how can we figure out how much the stuff they're giving us costs if we can't even figure out what it is?" Kevin asked.

"Yeah," Martha Jane said, "like that brown clump we get once in a while. I think it's supposed to be a dessert."

Lydia knew what she was talking about. "Right, the stuff with the white things in it. It might be rice pudding."

Emma shook her head. "I think those white things are coconut."

"All I know," Kevin added, "is that it stretches. And if you throw it on the floor, it'll bounce."

By now, they were all laughing. "Okay, okay," Lydia said. "But most of the stuff *is* recognizable, even if it's not edible. We could keep a record of everything they serve for a few days, and then . . ."

"And then what?" Emma asked.

Martha Jane clapped her hands together. "I know! I know!" she cried in glee.

"What?" they all chorused.

Martha Jane was so excited her words came out in a jumble. "My Aunt Andrea! She's a nutritionist and she knows *everything* about food. I'll bet if we give her a list of all the stuff they serve in the cafeteria for a few days, she can make up a list of foods that taste better, that are more nutritious, and that even cost the same!"

"Can she really do that?" Emma asked.

"Sure! She did it for my family. And believe me, we've been eating a lot better ever since."

"That's a fantastic idea!" Lydia exclaimed. "It's perfect! First we'll have the editorial about how bad the food is, and then we'll show them a typical menu that the cafeteria could serve instead."

"Then nobody can accuse us of just griping," Emma remarked.

"Absolutely," Kevin said. "We'll be showing the school how to do something better."

"And we'll be doing exactly what our newspaper is all about," Lydia added. "The *Alternative* presents . . . an alternative!"

Exactly one week later, Lydia was sitting at her desk, typing furiously. Martha Jane stood behind her, looking over her shoulder. "I'm glad we put those posters up at school," she said.

"I saw one across from my homeroom," Cassie said. She was sprawled on her bed, painting her nails. " 'The *Alternative* is coming. Watch out!' You made it sound like a monster's going to invade the school."

From the hallway came the sound of the phone ringing. Cassie started off the bed, then heard Daphne calling, "I'll get it!" She didn't sink back until it became obvious the call wasn't for her.

"It *is* like a monster," Lydia said, her fingers moving rapidly across the keys. "And it's going to devour Cedar Park Junior High." She paused to look over her work. "This is great—your aunt's got it all here. Amounts of protein, carbohydrates, everything."

"Aunt Andrea is a genius," Martha Jane said proudly. "And look—a serving of pasta primavera doesn't cost any more than those crummy hot dogs they feed us."

Cassie waved a hand in the air to dry. "Pasta primavera. That sounds fattening."

"It's just spaghetti with vegetables and cheese," Martha Jane explained. "My mother makes it all the time. It has fewer calories than hot dogs and it's better for you."

"Then I guess it couldn't taste very good," Cassie commented.

"There, it's finished," Lydia said. "Martha Jane, why don't you read it over and see if I made any mistakes."

She turned away from the typewriter and saw Daphne

standing tentatively in the doorway. Her expression looked funny—sort of pleased, sort of nervous.

"What's up?" Lydia asked. Daphne shuffled in and grinned sheepishly.

"Who was that on the phone?" Cassie asked.

Daphne adjusted her glasses self-consciously. "It was Rick Lewis. He wanted to know if I'd go to the ninth-grade dance with him."

"You're kidding!" Cassie practically screamed. "That's fabulous!" And then a look of despair crossed her face. "No, wait, this is awful! My younger sister, my seventh-grade sister, is going to the ninth-grade dance. I'm in the eighth grade and I don't even have a date!"

"What's the big deal?" Lydia asked. "I'm actually *in* the ninth grade and *I'm* not going to the dance."

"But you don't even want to go," Cassie wailed, "and I do."

Daphne sat down on the bed and put her hand on Cassie's shoulder as if to comfort her. "Maybe Zack will ask you. There's still time."

"I can't believe you guys," Lydia said scornfully. "All this fuss over a dumb dance."

"I'm going to the dance," Martha Jane said.

Lydia looked at her in surprise. Martha Jane had never been any more interested in dances than Lydia was. "You are?"

Martha Jane nodded. "With Kevin."

Now Lydia was truly amazed. "You and Kevin are *dating*? You didn't tell me that."

"Well, we're not exactly dating," Martha Jane said

hastily. "Just once in a while, we go places together. Like movies."

"That's called dating," Cassie said.

Lydia busied herself pulling the paper out of the typewriter and checking it again.

"I can take it over to the photocopy place now," Martha Jane offered. "Kevin said he'd meet me there."

Lydia handed the two sheets of paper to her and pretended not to notice the way Martha Jane flushed slightly when she said "Kevin." "Okay. And let's get to school early Monday so we can hand them out while people are coming in."

"Do you really think this newspaper is going to get us better food?" Cassie asked.

"Oh, probably not," Lydia said blithely. "But it's a way to get everyone interested. Then we'll start up petitions, put up posters, maybe even have a big rally."

Martha Jane's eyes widened. "Really?"

"Sure. And if that doesn't work, maybe we'll go on strike! We'll get everyone to stop buying lunch in the cafeteria and we can picket the principal's office!"

"Picket the principal's office . . . ," Martha Jane echoed weakly.

"Why not?" Lydia could see it all—the rallies, the pickets, the chanting of slogans like "We demand a decent lunch!" The image was dazzling.

She indicated the pages Martha Jane was clutching.

"This," she said dramatically, "is only the beginning!"

4

LYDIA DRESSED CAREFULLY Monday morning: black jeans, black turtleneck sweater, and a red bandanna tied around her head. She took a moment to admire herself in the mirror. With her short, jagged dark hair, her deep-set brown eyes burning with anticipation, she decided she looked tough—like someone who meant business. Which was exactly the way she felt.

Cassie, returning to the room after her shower, took one look at Lydia and shook her head in resignation. "Lydia, you don't care at all how you look, do you?"

" 'Course I care," Lydia replied. "Right now I look just like I want to look."

Cassie picked up her blow dryer and aimed it at her

head. "You'll never get a boyfriend if you go around looking like that."

Lydia gave a short laugh to indicate how much that dire prediction meant to her. Unfortunately, it couldn't be heard over the noise of the dryer.

"Who says I *want* a boyfriend?" she yelled. "I certainly don't want one like Zack Snyder."

That remark didn't seem to bother Cassie at all. "Haven't you ever had a crush on a boy?"

Lydia sat down on the bed and began pulling on her high-top black sneakers. "I don't *think* so. Not that I can remember, anyway."

Cassie turned off the dryer. "You'd know if you had one," she said wisely. "You feel all tingly and shaky, and you get little shivers in your stomach. Sometimes you feel dizzy, too. That's when you really know."

"Sounds like the flu," Lydia said. "See ya later." She grabbed her backpack and ran downstairs.

Her mother was in the kitchen, staring at a kettle on the stove. "A watched pot never boils, Mom," Lydia called out cheerfully as she reached into the refrigerator for a carton of orange juice.

"You're up early," Mrs. Gray noted, not bothering to stifle a yawn. "And I see you're dressed for battle."

Lydia quickly downed a glass of juice. "It's really exciting, Mom. You know, everyone complains about the food at school, but we're going to *do* something about it."

Her mother gazed at her warmly. "I think what you're doing is admirable. I just hope you won't be too disappointed if your newspaper doesn't make a big difference overnight."

"Oh, I won't," Lydia said quickly. "I've got all kinds of follow-up plans."

"You're not planning to blow up the cafeteria or anything like that, are you?"

"Not unless it's absolutely necessary," Lydia assured her. "And only as a last resort. Bye!"

She practically floated all the way to school. She felt positively giddy, like her whole body had goose pimples. It was sort of the feeling Cassie had described when she'd talked about having a crush. As far as Lydia was concerned, this had to be better. After all, who needed boys and dates and crushes when you had a great cause? One person could only care about so much.

Kevin and Martha Jane were waiting for her at the school entrance. Kevin held a stack of papers and Martha Jane was carrying two tall cups.

"What are the cups for?" Lydia asked.

"To collect the dimes. Take a look at the paper."

Lydia took the top sheet from Kevin's pile. Okay, maybe it didn't look like a traditional newspaper, but so what? The *Alternative* was definitely not traditional.

And there was her name, right on top: "Editor-in-Chief, Lydia Gray."

Emma arrived, and the group discussed strategy. "I think two of us should stay here," Lydia said, "and two should go to the side entrance."

"We'll go to the side," Martha Jane offered, and it was apparent the "we" meant she and Kevin. She took half the stack of papers and a cup, and the two hurried away.

Lydia turned to Emma. "Before the kids start arriving, we should drop a copy off at Mr. Fletcher's office."

"Now?" Emma looked more than a little apprehensive.

Lydia wondered if she was going to turn out to be a real ninny. "You can wait here," she said kindly. "I'll do it." She took a paper and ran into the school.

Her footsteps echoed in the deserted hallway. In the main office, a student helper sat behind the desk looking bored. "What do you want?" she asked Lydia suspiciously.

"Would you please see that Mr. Fletcher gets this right away?" Lydia asked sweetly.

The girl took the paper from her without even looking at it. Lydia waited a minute to make sure she put it in the box labeled *Principal* before she left.

"Did you give it to him?" Emma asked when she returned.

"It's in his box," Lydia said, looking out at the parking lot. Some cars were entering and discharging kids. "I'll probably get called to the principal's office later," she added, trying to sound casual and unconcerned.

"If you want," Emma said bravely, "I'll go with you."

Lydia shook her head. She still didn't know that much about Emma—she just might be the type who would break down and cry and say she was sorry. "I can handle it."

Some students were approaching the entrance, and Lydia got to work. "Get your copy of the *Alternative!* Only ten cents! Find out what's really going on!"

"Buy the *Alternative!*" Emma echoed.

Kevin had been right. Most of the kids had a dime in their pockets. Curiosity, if nothing else, got them to turn those dimes over to Emma and Lydia.

"Here comes George Philips," Lydia muttered to Emma. "Watch this." She beamed at the *Century* editor. "Hi, George! Want an *Alternative?* It's only a dime."

The portly boy replied jovially. "I guess it's worth a dime to check out the competition." A slight twist to his lips made it clear he didn't really think the *Alternative* could be competition at all. Lydia didn't care. She enjoyed the image of his eyes popping out when he actually read the newspaper.

"Want to buy an *Alternative?*" she asked a girl walking by. The girl glanced at the paper.

"What is it?"

"It's a newspaper."

The girl squinted. "It doesn't look like a newspaper."

"Well, it *is*," Lydia said impatiently. "Do you want it or don't you? It's only ten cents, and it's all about how we can get better lunches in the cafeteria."

"I bring my lunch."

Lydia waved a hand to dismiss her and turned to the next group walking in. "Want to buy the *Alternative?*" When she completed her transaction, she noticed that the girl was still standing there, looking pensive.

"Of course," she said, "if the food here was better, I wouldn't have to pack my lunch every morning." Her forehead wrinkled, then cleared as she ultimately came to a decision. "Okay." She handed Lydia a dime.

"Boy, if that's what she goes through to spend a dime,

can you imagine what happens if she has to spend a dollar?"

Emma wasn't listening. She was busy arguing with a boy. "No returns. Sorry."

"What a rip-off," the boy muttered. On closer inspection, Lydia realized he was Zack Snyder, Cassie's latest passion.

"How about an exchange?" Zack asked.

Emma raised her eyes in exasperation. "There's nothing to exchange it for!"

Zack snickered. "Sure there is. How about you?"

"Huh?"

"I give you back the paper, and you go to the ninth-grade dance with me." He looked very pleased with his clever notion. Emma didn't appear impressed.

"Sorry, I've got a date," she said shortly, turning to some other kids who were approaching the entrance.

Zack crumpled up his *Alternative* and tossed it over his shoulder. "Wouldn't have spent more than a dime on you anyway."

What a creep, Lydia thought. What did Cassie see in him? She tried to look at him objectively. With his shiny black hair and broad shoulders, she supposed he was kind of handsome. But he looked like the type who would think so, too.

"Got any more papers?" Emma asked. "I'm all out."

With a start, Lydia realized she only had two left. "I'm buying them," she said, sticking her hand in her pocket. She pulled out a quarter, put it in the cup, extracted a nickel, and grinned triumphantly. "There! Now we're sold out."

Emma picked up a cup. "Not bad for our first issue. Now what happens?"

"Depends," Lydia said as they walked into the building. "Did you know that practically every revolution started with the printed word? A newspaper, or a book . . ."

Emma gave her an uneasy sideways glance. "I don't know if I'm up for a revolution."

Lydia patted her shoulder. "Don't worry. It'll be nonviolent. See ya later." She raced off to her homeroom, wondering if anyone would be talking about the *Alternative*.

The response was better than anything she could have dreamed. All morning kids stopped her in the halls and came up to her in classes. In different ways, they all said pretty much the same thing: "It's about time somebody did something about that trash they call food!"

The *Alternative* had obviously struck a nerve in the heart of Cedar Park Junior High. People she didn't even know congratulated her.

Even her English teacher remarked on it. "This is very interesting, Lydia. You present an excellent argument. I've always thought the cafeteria could stand a bit of improvement, but I had no idea it could be done so cheaply."

"Thank you," Lydia said, with an attempt to sound modest. It wasn't easy. She had noticed kids pointing her out in the halls. She was famous! And this was only the beginning.

It was during history, right before lunch, that the

message she was expecting came over the intercom. "Would Lydia Gray please come to the office?"

Martha Jane was sitting three rows in front of her. She turned and looked at Lydia, her eyes wide and eyebrows way up. Lydia rose calmly and went up the aisle. As she passed Martha Jane, her friend whispered, "Want me to come with you?" Lydia mouthed "No," accepted a pass from the teacher, and walked out of the room.

With her head high and shoulders back, she proceeded up the hall and turned left sharply. She felt like a soldier, she felt like Joan of Arc—not going to the stake, but on her way to lead an army.

The regular secretary was in the office this time. "Yes?"

"I'm Lydia Gray. I think Mr. Fletcher wants to see me."

"Oh, yes. One moment." She picked up a phone and pressed a button. "Mr. Fletcher? Lydia Gray is here." She listened for a second, then put the phone down. "You can go right on in." Lydia thought she could actually hear her heart pounding as she tapped lightly on the door and turned the knob.

The slightly bald, slender man behind the massive desk rose as she entered. "Come in, come in," he said, smiling warmly. Lydia wasn't fooled. He was probably going to try to sweet-talk her. Well, he didn't know who he was dealing with. What could he make her do anyway? Recall the newspapers?

Mr. Fletcher held up the *Alternative*. "I understand you're in charge of this."

"Yes, I am," Lydia replied, pride ringing in every word.

"Very interesting." He sat down and leaned back in his chair. "Funny, I had no idea—"

"—that the food was so terrible?" Lydia finished. She half rose from her chair. "Well, it is, Mr. Fletcher. And I think I speak for all the students when I say something should be done about it."

"I agree," Mr. Fletcher said. "Lydia, you don't have to tell me how bad the food is. I *know* how bad it is. Why do you think I do this?" He reached into a drawer and withdrew a brown paper bag.

Lydia sank back in her seat. "Oh."

"What I was about to say was that I had no idea we could have, uh—" he checked the *Alternative* "—that we could have quiche lorraine for the same price as tuna surprise."

"And it's better for us, too," Lydia supplied.

"I see that. I want you to know that I called the superintendent's office this morning and she agreed to bring in a professional nutrition consultant. We're going to look into overhauling our entire meal service." He paused, as if giving this time to sink in.

Lydia just sat there. She couldn't quite believe what she was hearing.

Mr. Fletcher looked a little surprised by her reaction— or lack of it. "Well? What do you think of that?"

Lydia found her voice. "Uh, that's great."

The bell rang, and Mr. Fletcher got up. Lydia rose too. He extended his right hand, and she automatically shook it.

"I'd like to thank you and your staff for your fine work in bringing this to our attention. Now, you better hurry or you'll be late for lunch. Not that it's worth being on time for." He laughed heartily at his own joke. Lydia could only manage a feeble half-grin.

She left the office in a fog. She'd won! Hastily, she amended that: the *Alternative* had won! Four ordinary ninth graders had just accomplished a goal that would change the lives of the entire student body. Amazing!

And it had been so easy. Which was nice in a way . . . sort of like playing Scrabble with Phoebe. Fee was three years younger, and Lydia could always beat her. No sweat.

For a few brief seconds, her excitement dimmed. Had it been *too* easy? What happened to her plans for rallies and protest marches and strikes?

Resolutely, she pushed any tiny trace of disappointment aside. There'd be other causes, other campaigns where she'd have to fight harder. Right now, she might as well bask in the glow of this major victory—even if it hadn't been much of a battle.

5

LIKE A TRIUMPHANT GENERAL, Lydia marched into the cafeteria, headed directly toward the table where Martha Jane, Kevin, and Emma were sitting, and announced the good news. Martha Jane's shriek of joy could actually be heard over the cafeteria din. The general excitement at the table even attracted several other kids.

"What's going on?" one boy asked.

"Mr. Fletcher says the *Alternative*'s right!" Kevin announced loudly. "We're actually going to get better food!"

The boy slapped Lydia on the back. "Hey, al-right!"

A crowd started to gather around the table, and as they heard the news, Lydia and the rest of the staff were treated to congratulations and cheers. Kids Lydia didn't even know were heaping praise on the *Alternative*.

"This is just what we needed," a girl exclaimed. "You guys have clout! You can make some real changes at this school!"

Lydia smiled modestly. "I guess the electric typewriter is mightier than the sword."

"Wait till you see what we do next!" Kevin called to the crowd as they started to disperse.

"We're off to a great start," Emma said with satisfaction. "And we've got plenty of money to run off the next issue."

"And now that we've established a reputation for getting things done, everyone will buy it," Martha Jane added.

Lydia plunked her elbows on the table and rested her chin in her hands. "But what *are* we going to do next?"

"We'll think of something," Kevin said airily. "Right now I think we should be talking about a celebration. Not only is the *Alternative* a smashing success, we've actually done a major good deed for this school."

"No kidding," Martha Jane said, eyeing the day's main course with unconcealed distaste.

Emma gazed dreamily at her plate. "Just think. Someday soon, this is going to be curried chicken salad. Or fettucine Alfredo."

"But right now it's still Salisbury steak." Martha Jane's tone was mournful. "And I'm starving."

Lydia picked up a fork and tried to cut the lump of meat. After several futile attempts, she put the fork down and scowled at the plate. "I don't think I could ever be hungry enough to eat this."

"Don't think about it," Kevin advised her. "Think about pizza, oozing with sauce and sticky cheese, covered with pepperoni—"

"Stop, stop!" Martha Jane wailed. "You're killing me."

Kevin smiled benignly. "So how about having our celebration right after school today at Gino's Pizza Parlor?"

"Sounds good to me," Lydia said.

Kevin turned to Martha Jane. "You're not working out today, are you?"

"No, I went to the gym yesterday. I'm not supposed to work out two days in a row."

"What do you actually do in your workouts?" Lydia asked her.

"Weightlifting," Martha Jane replied. "I've been doing it for three months now. Look!" She pushed back the sleeve of her sweater and flexed her arm.

"Wow!" Emma exclaimed. "You've got real muscles!"

Kevin grinned proudly. "I'll bet Martha Jane could beat up a guy twice her size."

Martha Jane gave him a sidelong glance. "That's probably why you hang out with me. For protection."

The image of Martha Jane defending the rather slender, definitely nonathletic Kevin from some hulking brute sent everyone off into gales of laughter.

Lydia was laughing with the rest of them, but her thoughts were elsewhere. "You know, guys, we really do have to come up with something awfully good for the next issue. We better start talking about it."

"We've got plenty of possible topics," Emma said.

Kevin agreed. "Sure, any one of them will do. And

there's no reason why we can't talk about it over pizza this afternoon."

"Okay," Lydia said, but she wondered how much serious work could be done in a pizza parlor. "I've got to get to class."

"Me too," Emma said. "I'll walk with you."

They were just leaving the cafeteria when a boy coming in called out to Emma.

"Here's that book you wanted to borrow. Can you get it back to me after school?"

"Sure," Emma said. She took the book from the boy and then the two of them stood there for a moment, silently, smiling at each other. Finally Emma said, "I'll see you later," and rejoined Lydia.

"Who was that?" Lydia asked.

"Joshua Campbell. He just transferred here this year." She paused and blushed slightly. "That's who I'm going to the ninth-grade dance with."

"You really have a date?" Lydia asked in surprise. "I thought you just said that this morning to get out of going with Zack."

"Oh, no," Emma said. "I've been seeing Joshua for the past month. He's cute, don't you think?"

"I guess so." Lydia began to wonder if she was the only ninth grader not going to the dance. Not that she really cared, but . . .

"And he's on the football team," Emma continued. "Of course, that's nothing to brag about. They haven't won a game all season."

Lydia was only half-listening. She told Emma she'd see her after school. Moments later, she slipped into her geometry class just seconds before the bell. The teacher was busily drawing triangles on the board and Lydia let her thoughts drift.

She'd never thought much about stuff like dances before. As for boys and dates, they'd never concerned her either. Of course, she had friends who were boys—Kevin, for example. But she couldn't remember ever having any special interest in them—certainly not the way Cassie did.

It didn't really bother her that most of her friends now had boyfriends. She always liked being different. And it wasn't as if she was adamantly opposed to the idea of a boyfriend. If she ever met a boy who made her feel the way Cassie had described, she supposed she wouldn't mind. But a girl couldn't force herself to feel tingles, could she?

"Lydia!"

She looked up and blinked. The teacher was staring at her, hands on her hips.

"That's the third time I've had to say your name."

"I guess I wasn't paying attention."

"Would it be too much to ask you to take your mind off pasta primavera for a few moments and concentrate on geometry?" Her voice was firm but her eyes were smiling.

Lydia was actually relieved to push the troublesome thoughts from her mind. "Sorry," she said meekly, focusing on the board.

When the bell rang, Ben McGillis, who sat in front of her, turned around. "Hey, that newspaper of yours is great. I heard Mr. Fletcher was really impressed. Is he going to do something about the food?"

"That's what he says," Lydia told him. She found herself looking Ben over carefully. Reddish brown hair, nice white teeth—could he be someone she might be interested in?

"What are you going to write about next?"

"We're not sure yet," Lydia replied carefully. "What do you think about the honor code?"

He looked at her blankly. "What about it?"

"Well, some kids think it's not fair. You know, the part about how we're supposed to turn in kids we see cheating."

Ben shrugged. "I guess I never saw anyone cheating. Besides, the teachers usually catch them anyway. Is that what's going to be in the next *Alternative*?" He sounded disappointed.

"Not necessarily," Lydia said hastily. "It was just an idea."

"Hope you come up with something better than that," Ben said, grabbing his books.

Lydia watched him leave and waited to see if she was feeling anything. No tingles. Nothing even remotely resembling them. She shrugged it off, gathered her books, and left the room.

She had just started down the hall when she saw Cassie and Daphne running toward her.

"I heard you get called to the office!" Cassie said breathlessly. "What happened?"

Daphne looked anxious. "I hope you didn't get into any trouble."

"Not a bit," Lydia said smugly. "As a matter of fact, Mr. Fletcher was so impressed with the newspaper that he's actually seeing about having the food changed."

Daphne's face lit up. "Oh, Lydia, that's wonderful! Wait till Mom and Dad hear about this."

Even Cassie had the courtesy to look impressed. "You can do that with one dumb newspaper? Wow, now maybe you can ask for something *really* important."

"Got any ideas?"

Daphne pushed her glasses back up her nose and looked at Lydia earnestly. "Do you think maybe you could ask for more advanced English courses? Like, a whole course on Edna St. Vincent Millay?"

Lydia smiled at her kindly. "I don't think that's the kind of subject a lot of kids would go wild about."

"No kidding," Cassie snorted. "I've never even heard of this Edna person. Now, *I've* got an idea everyone could get into. At least, all the girls."

"What is it?"

"New mirrors for the girls' locker room! The kind with lights all around. It's absolutely impossible to put your makeup on right in those crummy mirrors."

Lydia groaned. "Yeah, that's a real serious problem, Cassie."

As usual, her sarcasm had no effect whatsoever. "Hey, I saw Zack today," Cassie said, hugging her books tightly, "and he *talked* to me. I still think he's maybe going to ask me to the dance."

Lydia bit her lip. Should she tell Cassie that he'd already asked Emma first? No, she didn't really want to deal with Cassie's hysterics right there in the middle of the hall.

"That's nice," she said. "Look, tell Mom I'll be home a little late, okay? I'm going out for pizza with Martha Jane and the others to celebrate."

Cassie shook her head sadly. "Pizza. Do you know how many calories are in one slice of pizza?"

"Lydia doesn't have to worry about calories," Daphne said loyally. She looked up at her oldest sister with a wistful expression. "Lydia, I wish you were going to the dance, too. I feel sort of funny being a seventh grader and going to a ninth-grade dance. I think I'd feel better if you were there."

"*I'll* be there," Cassie interjected. "Hopefully."

Lydia patted Daphne on the shoulder. "You'll be fine. I've gotta go. See you at home."

As the afternoon progressed, the word spread through the school that Mr. Fletcher was actually going to follow the advice of the *Alternative*. In each of her classes, Lydia was congratulated. In one class, the students even gave her a round of applause.

She felt like a real hero. But all the while, she dreaded the inevitable question that came after the congratulations: What are you going to do next? Honor codes, Junior Princess, cheerleading—none of the other topics had the pizzazz of cafeteria food. The honor code was boring, the Junior Princess contest was way off in the spring, and most kids didn't care that much about cheerleaders.

If they couldn't find a popular topic, they at least had

to come up with a controversial one—something that wouldn't be a letdown after their big success.

The gang was waiting for her after school at the entrance. They were all in a festive mood.

"I've never felt so popular in my life," Martha Jane said. "Do you know, some kids actually *thanked* me!"

"I feel like the whole school is thanking us," Kevin exclaimed. He turned, looked back at the building, and extended his arms. "You're welcome!"

"Guys, we really have to think about our next issue," Lydia said loudly, hoping to bring them back down to earth. "People are going to be expecting big things from us."

"I think we deserve an award," Kevin said. "But I'll settle for a giant pizza with everything."

"Can we walk by the football field?" Emma asked. "I have to return this book."

"Listen," Lydia pleaded as they ambled over toward the field, "I'm serious. What are we going to do next?"

Kevin sighed. "Can't we just rest on our laurels for a while?"

"No, no," Lydia said vehemently. "We've caught their interest now, and we can't lose it. We have to come up with something that's really startling."

They stood at the edge of the football field where the Panthers were gathering for practice. A few guys were tossing balls back and forth. They seemed to be throwing them okay. However, no one seemed to be able to catch them.

Joshua, Emma's friend, saw them and waved. With another player, he strolled over toward them. Lydia recognized the other boy—Sam something. Keller? Kelly? He'd been in one of her classes last year.

Emma introduced Joshua to the others. "And I guess you know Sam Kelsey. He's cocaptain."

"Hi," Sam said. He brushed curly brown hair out of his eyes and looked at Lydia. "You were in my social studies class last year."

It was more a statement than a question, so Lydia just nodded.

Sam grinned at her. "I remember when you gave that report on communal living experiments. Someone in class called you a communist."

"I remember," Lydia said shortly. It wasn't one of her more pleasant memories of eighth grade.

Sam didn't seem put off by her tone. "Were you the one who came up with the *Alternative*?"

"It was all of us together."

"But it was definitely Lydia's idea first," Martha Jane supplied.

"Great idea," Sam said. Lydia wondered if that smile was permanently fixed to his face.

"C'mon! Let's get going!" Zack Snyder was yelling to the boys from the field.

"See you later," Sam said generally, but his eyes were on Lydia. She wasn't sorry to see him go. That smile was beginning to make her feel uncomfortable.

They watched while the players got into a formation and began a play. After a few seconds, Kevin said what they were all thinking. "Boy, are they lousy."

"Pretty pathetic," Martha Jane agreed.

Emma tried to defend them. "I think it's because

most of them are pretty small. Except for Joshua and Sam and Zack. They're just not all that strong."

"What they need is Martha Jane on the team," Kevin said. "C'mon, let's go get that pizza."

Lydia didn't move.

"Lydia?" Martha Jane was staring at her. "Are you okay?"

Lydia felt a tingle run through her—a tingle she recognized. She felt like one of those cartoon characters with a light bulb over her head. Only this time, it felt more like a lightning bolt.

"How's this for our next headline?" She faced the others, hoping her excitement wouldn't make her voice tremble. " 'What This Football Team Needs Is a Few Good Women!' "

6

GIRLS ON THE FOOTBALL TEAM?" Martha Jane looked pensive as she took another bite of pizza. She chewed slowly, her forehead creased and her eyes squinting—a clear indication that the idea didn't exactly thrill her. Finally she swallowed and spoke again. "I don't know, Lydia. Isn't that sort of unrealistic?"

Lydia leaned forward. "What's unrealistic about it? Why shouldn't girls be allowed to go out for football?"

Emma's expression was doubtful, too. "I've never heard of mixing sexes on a team."

Lydia shrugged. "Just because it hasn't been done before doesn't mean it can't be done."

At least Kevin didn't look so skeptical. "It *has* been done before. You ever heard of the Harlem Globetrotters? The famous basketball players? There's a woman on the team."

Emma still didn't appear too enthusiastic. She picked off a piece of pepperoni and popped it in her mouth. "I don't know any girls who even want to play football."

"That's just because they've never thought about it," Lydia argued. "And besides, that's not even the point. It's the principle of the thing. All I want is for girls to have the right to play football if they want to."

"I agree," Kevin said. "If girls have the qualifications, why shouldn't they be allowed to try out for the Panthers? I think this is an excellent challenge for the *Alternative* to take on. It's a lot different than complaining about food in the cafeteria, and it'll grab everyone's attention."

Martha Jane's forehead had cleared, but she still didn't look particularly convinced. "It won't be as popular, either. And I'll bet anything Mr. Fletcher won't be too crazy about the idea."

"So what?" Lydia asked. "The *Alternative* shouldn't be afraid to take on unpopular issues. We can't always expect the principal to be on our side."

"It's not just the principal," Emma warned. "Some kids are going to think it's a terrible idea."

"But that's what makes it interesting!" Lydia said. "It's controversial!"

Martha Jane separated a string of cheese that hung suspended between her mouth and her slice. "If Mr. Fletcher really disapproved, we'd have a great headline for a follow-up issue—'The Principal vs. the Principle'!"

"And I'll bet we do get a lot of kids on our side,"

54

Kevin noted. "There are probably a bunch of girls, athletic types, who have a secret longing to play football."

Martha Jane cocked her head to one side. "I guess it could be kind of interesting to see what happens. . . ."

Lydia looked at her hopefully. Was there a hint of enthusiasm in her voice?

Emma giggled, and Lydia looked at her. "What's so funny?"

"I just had this image of me tackling Joshua."

Lydia groaned and turned her attention to Martha Jane. She was nodding slowly.

"You know, I'm starting to see possibilities in this. If we focused in on the equal opportunity angle—"

"That's it," Kevin interrupted. "The school is supported by taxes, right? And everyone's parents have to pay taxes. So every student should be allowed the right to participate in all school activities!"

"Exactly!" Lydia exclaimed.

Now Martha Jane was sitting up straight, her eyes bright. "This could actually be exciting! We could make history!"

Pleased, Lydia allowed herself to relax and lean back in her seat. "Then we're all in agreement?"

"Absolutely," Kevin and Martha Jane chorused. They all turned to Emma.

"I guess so," she said uncertainly. "I'm just not sure what Joshua will think of this."

"Why does it matter what Joshua thinks?" Lydia demanded. Emma didn't reply, but she didn't need to— Lydia already knew the reason. Girls got involved with boys romantically and then they let the boys tell them what to do. She'd seen it happen to Cassie a zillion times. It was just one more good reason not to have a boyfriend. Unless Joshua agreed that girls had the right to play football, Lydia had a feeling Emma wouldn't be playing a very active role in the creation of the next week's *Alternative*.

"Let's decide what we're going to include in the paper," she said briskly, pulling a notebook out of her backpack.

"How about if Kevin and I do a survey of students?" Martha Jane suggested. "Something like, 'Girls should have the right to try out for the football team—yes or no?' We could pass them out tomorrow after school."

"And we'll get some comments from them we can quote in the article," Kevin added.

"Good," Lydia said, writing it down. "Maybe I should do some interviews. Like with Coach Benson. I had him for social studies last year and I think he might remember me."

"And maybe you should interview some of the players, too," Kevin said. "The captain, for example. Who *is* the captain, anyway?"

"Zack Snyder," Lydia murmured, making a face. That was one person she wasn't looking forward to interviewing.

"He's cocaptain," Martha Jane said. "The other one is Sam what's-his-name."

"Kelsey," Lydia said, making a note of it. "What do you want to do, Emma?"

Emma was silent for a moment. "I guess," she began

slowly, "I could do some background stuff. You know, girls who have been important athletes."

"If we can pull this off," Martha Jane mused, "we could make Cedar Park Junior High famous."

Kevin nodded as he reached for the last slice. "It's definitely going to cause an uproar. I can't wait to hear some of the reactions!"

"Girls on the football team?" Lydia's father sat up and looked at her as if she had quite simply lost her mind.

Lydia plunked down on the sofa next to him. "Why not?"

Her mother looked up from her chair and peered at Mr. Gray keenly. "Yes, David, why not?"

Mr. Gray seemed to have some difficulty coming up with a response. "It's . . . it's . . . I don't know, it's just—"

Lydia grinned at him. "See? There's absolutely no reason why girls shouldn't be allowed to play football."

"Yes, there is! Girls aren't physically built to play football. That's all there is to it, and there's not a thing you can do about it. It's a fact of nature." Mr. Gray leaned back triumphantly.

"Dad, we're not talking about the Chicago Bears. Have you ever seen the Panthers? Those guys are positively puny. At least, most of them are."

"That's a good point," Mrs. Gray remarked. "At your age, girls do tend to be more physically mature than boys. It's also a fact of nature," she added slyly.

"But—*football?*" Mr. Gray looked mournful. "It's one of the last bastions of male exclusivity."

Lydia blinked. "Huh?"

"What your father is saying," Mrs. Gray said, her eyes narrowing, "is that it's one of the few activities in the world that's totally closed to women. Seriously, David, why shouldn't junior high girls play football? If they have the appropriate physical qualifications and the talent to do whatever it is football players have to do, I can't see any reason why they shouldn't be allowed to compete."

"Dad, you sound like a sexist," Lydia stated.

Mr. Gray looked offended. "Hey, come on. You know I'm completely in favor of equal rights and equal opportunity. And I'm very glad to see women becoming doctors and lawyers and astronauts and everything else. But, *football* . . . ," he sighed, shaking his head. Lydia could swear his eyes were actually getting misty. "Football is more than just a game. It's a tradition. It's got a special meaning for men. It's a shared experience, it gives them a bond."

"Really?" Mrs. Gray asked with a dangerous smile. "Like housework for women?"

"Or cooking?" Lydia tossed in.

"Oh, Lois," Mr. Gray groaned. "You and Lydia don't understand. And that's just my point. Women don't understand the true meaning and significance of football."

Mrs. Gray brushed that aside. "All I understand is that you're making something mystical and romantic out of a bunch of overdeveloped hulking men tossing a ball and chasing after it. And Lydia's talking about opening doors that have been closed to women." She smiled warmly at her oldest daughter. "Personally, I'm very proud of you."

"Thanks, Mom." Lydia turned to her father. "How about you? Aren't you proud of me?"

Mr. Gray put up his hands in mock surrender. "Okay, okay, I give up. Yes, I'm proud of you. I'm always happy to see you stand up for what you believe in." His next words seemed to require a monumental effort. "And I suppose, on a philosophical basis, I have to agree with you."

"I knew it!" Mrs. Gray said gleefully. "Any person who's written as many editorials as you have on equal rights for women has to agree."

Casually, Lydia examined her slightly chewed finger-nails. "If that's really true, Dad, how about writing an editorial about this?"

"Pro or con?"

"Dad!"

He gave her an apologetic grin. "I hardly think it would be ethical for me to write an editorial about my own daughter's campaign. However, I suppose if anything newsworthy comes of it, we'll have to give it a mention." He leaned over and ruffled her hair. "How's this—I'll let a reporter know what you guys are up to, okay?"

"Great! We'll need all the publicity we can get!"

Phoebe wandered into the room and addressed the group in general. "Is it time for dinner yet?"

Mrs. Gray tossed her a meaningful look. "It will be once the table's set."

"Oh. Okay." She started toward the kitchen but Mr. Gray stopped her.

"What do you think of your sister's latest revolution? She wants to put girls on the junior high football team."

Phoebe's eyes widened. "Is that what you're going to do?"

"We're going to try." Lydia told her.

"Wow. First you get them to change the cafeteria food, and now you're going to make them put girls on the football team." She gazed at Lydia with an expression that was just short of worshipful.

"She's not going to *make* anyone do anything," Mrs. Gray said quickly. "She's going to *suggest*."

That didn't seem to affect Phoebe's opinion. "I'll bet she can do it, too."

Lydia beamed at her. There was nothing like having a kid sister who thought you were wonderful to make you feel like you could do absolutely anything. "See?" she pointed out to her father. "A lot of kids are going to support us."

"Don't be so sure of that," Mr. Gray replied. "I have a pretty good feeling some of the boys might resent this."

"I know that," Lydia said. "But the girls will back us. And that's just about fifty percent of the student body right there."

Mrs. Gray raised her eyebrows. "I don't think you'll get much support from Cassie."

Lydia grinned. "You never know. She might even want to try out for the team herself. It would be a way for her to meet more football players!"

Phoebe didn't agree. "She'd never go out for football. She might get her hair messed up."

"Have you had any feedback from other students yet?" Mrs. Gray asked.

Lydia shook her head. "Martha Jane and Kevin are going to do a survey. And tomorrow I'm going to try to interview some of the team. And Coach Benson, too."

"I wonder how *he's* going to respond," her father mused.

Lydia shrugged. "Oh, he probably won't like the idea right off. But I bet I'll be able to convince him."

"You think so?" Mr. Gray's expression was doubtful.

"Sure," Lydia replied with confidence. "I convinced you, didn't I?"

Her father acknowledged this with a grin and another ruffle of her hair. But he still looked doubtful.

"Girls on the football team?" The eyebrows of the heavyset football coach shot up so high they practically met his receding hairline.

"Sure!" Without waiting for an invitation, Lydia plunked down on the chair next to his desk. "We—the staff of the *Alternative*, that is—think the female students at Cedar Park Junior High should have the right to go out for football. Now, what's your opinion?" Poised with her pen gripped tightly in her hand, she waited to put his response on paper.

Coach Benson looked at her blankly for a moment. Then he started shuffling papers on his desk. "This is all very amusing, young lady, but I'm a very busy man and I don't have time for your little jokes."

Lydia moved her chair closer in an attempt to establish eye contact. "It's not a joke, Coach," she said earnestly. "We're very serious. It's a question of equal opportunity and equal rights and—"

"Nonsense," the coach interrupted. "You don't mix the sexes on an athletic team."

"Oh, yeah?" Lydia tried not to sound too belligerent. It wouldn't help to alienate him. "Haven't you ever heard of the Harlem Globetrotters?"

"That's basketball. Football's a much more physical sport. There's body contact, and it can get pretty rough. Girls couldn't handle that."

Lydia sniffed. "Did you ever watch girls play hockey? They're positively brutal."

Coach Benson looked like he was trying very hard to retain his patience. "That's girls playing with girls. Girls can't play with boys on the same team. They don't have the physical strength—"

"Some of them do," Lydia interjected. "There are lots of ninth-grade girls who are bigger than the boys—and stronger, too."

The coach acted like he hadn't even heard her. "And they don't have the endurance or the competitive edge. That's what makes a winning team."

"A winning team," Lydia repeated as she scrambled to get that down on paper. "Like the Cedar Park Panthers?"

Even as she spoke, she regretted her sarcasm. She had a feeling the coach wouldn't appreciate it. She was right. His face was turning beet red.

"I've had enough of this nonsense. Now run along before you're late for class."

His casual dismissal infuriated her, but she gritted her teeth to keep from expressing her feelings. After all, he was a teacher as well as the coach. But she couldn't resist a parting shot.

"Coach Benson, I'm sorry you think this is nonsense. The *Alternative* believes it's one more step in the battle for women's rights. We are appealing to the student body for support. Maybe a boycott of the football games will convince you this isn't nonsense."

For a second she thought maybe she'd gone too far. You weren't supposed to threaten teachers. But the coach only looked at her quizzically.

"Aren't you the girl who gave a report in my class last year about communist living?"

Lydia corrected him. "Communal living experiments."

He grunted. "It figures."

Lydia was about to ask him what he'd meant by that when the bell rang. Without so much as a thank you for his time, she turned and walked out the door.

Maybe she'd have better luck with the cocaptains.

"Girls on the football team?" At first, Zack's expression was incredulous. Then he started laughing.

"What's so funny about that?" Lydia demanded. She'd been waiting outside the boys' locker room for over half an hour and wasn't in the best of moods. Three times that day, in casual conversations with friends, she'd brought up her idea. And all three of them had responded with the same look of disbelief and the same question: "Girls on the football team?"

And now this jerk was laughing.

"You gotta be kidding," Zack sneered. "No way."

Lydia balanced her open notebook in one hand and her pen in the other. "Is that what you want me to quote you as saying?"

"Write whatever you want," Zack replied. "Everyone's going to be laughing too hard to read it anyway."

Lydia eyed him coldly. "Right now, at this very moment, two reporters are in front of school passing out surveys. When we publish the results, maybe you won't think this is so funny."

"Oh, yeah? Maybe I'll just have to conduct my own survey." He called out to two members of the team who had just emerged from the locker room. "Hey, guys— come here."

The boys ambled over. "What's up?" one of them asked.

"Lydia here wants to know what we think of letting girls go out for football."

"Hey, that's not a bad idea," one player said.

Lydia smiled.

"I can think of a couple of girls I wouldn't mind getting into a huddle with," he continued, with an exaggerated leer.

Her smile disappeared and she could feel her face going red as the three boys laughed. "For your information," she stated, her voice rising with each word, "there are girls in this school who can run faster and throw harder than any boy. And they're bigger than you are, too."

"Oh, yeah?" one boy responded. "Maybe they should go on a diet." That set the three of them off laughing again.

Lydia noticed that the knuckles on her hand gripping the pen were turning white. She felt like she was going to explode. These creeps weren't even willing to listen!

Zack finally stopped laughing. Scrutinizing Lydia curiously, he asked, "You're Cassie's sister, right?"

"Yes," Lydia snapped. "What's that got to do with anything?"

"I was just wondering how a cute girl like that could have such a wacko sister." With that, he joined his buddies and the three of them sauntered out the door. Lydia stared after them in anger and dismay.

"Hi!"

Lydia almost jumped. She turned and saw Sam Kelsey standing there, grinning at her. She didn't bother to return the greeting. Pen in position, she put forth her question. "What's your opinion of girls trying out for the football team?"

Sam looked taken aback. "Girls? On the football team?"

"Oh, never mind!" Leaving a slightly bewildered football player in her wake, she whirled around and stormed out the door.

7

"Lydia, could you hand me a tissue, please?" Martha Jane croaked.

Lydia's hand left the typewriter keys only long enough to pull a tissue from the box on her desk and hold it over her shoulder.

"Thanks." Martha Jane's voice was muffled as she blew her nose. Lydia kept her eyes firmly fixed on the almost blank paper that stuck out from the typewriter. For three days in a row she'd been trying to write up this interview. Now it was Thursday evening and this was her zillionth attempt to get it right.

She finished typing the sentence she'd started. "How does this sound? 'When I asked Zack Snyder what he thought of our idea, he had little to say. It was clear that he lacked the intelligence to understand the question.' "

Martha Jane leaned over Lydia's shoulder so she could read the passage herself. "I don't know, Lydia. That's kind of strong, isn't it? I mean, you don't really know that he's not intelligent."

In Lydia's opinion, it was a perfectly logical statement. "If you could have heard the way he laughed at me, you'd know he can't be too smart. Maybe I should have said 'he *seemed* to lack the intelligence to understand the question.' Is that any better?"

A series of coughs was Martha Jane's only response.

"You see," Lydia continued, "when you write up an interview, you have to make the people who say negative things sound stupid. That way no one will trust their opinion."

Martha Jane gasped, a noise alarming enough to make Lydia actually turn around and look at her. Her friend held a finger under her nose. "Quick—a tissue!"

Hastily, Lydia grabbed the whole box and thrust it at her. Martha Jane sneezed three times in rapid succession. Lydia frowned. "I hope you're not getting sick. We've got a lot of work to do if we're going to have this issue ready for next week."

Martha Jane put a hand to her forehead. "I feel warm," she said worriedly.

"Don't think about it," Lydia advised her. "Mind over matter. Maybe it will just go away." She took a piece of paper from her desk. "Listen to this: 'Although Coach Benson admitted there were some problems that had to be overcome before girls could take an active part in

67

playing football, he showed a great deal of interest in the idea.' "

Martha Jane made a face. "Come on, Lydia. You make it sound like he's in favor of it. That's not the way you described it to me."

Lydia tossed the paper back onto the desk. "We've got to have *somebody* saying *something* positive in this issue. Otherwise it's going to sound like we're the only ones in favor of it."

Martha Jane sniffled and wiped her nose. "I hate to break it to you, but I think we are. You read the comments on the surveys we passed out." She grabbed a folder lying on the bed and withdrew a few sheets of paper. " 'This is a really stupid idea.' " She put one sheet down. " 'The uniforms wouldn't fit them,' " she read from the next. " 'The Panthers are bad enough already. Do you really think girls would improve the team?' "

"Okay, okay," Lydia said. "I know what they say—I read them. But I've been thinking: maybe we could still use some of the comments, if we only use part of them. Like, 'Girls would improve the team.' "

Martha Jane started sneezing again. Between sneezes, she managed to say, "I don't think that's honest."

Lydia had to agree. "I guess not. Well, we'll just have to use the *Alternative* to change their minds. How many responses did you get, anyway?"

"About fifty. We passed out a hundred."

"And there are almost 400 kids in that school. That's at least 350 kids who might not even have an opinion yet. All we have to do is make a good case and convince them it's a good idea."

"But how are we going to do that?" Martha Jane asked plaintively.

"Well, there's Emma's report on girls and sports. . . ."

Martha Jane took another tissue and blew her nose. "I wouldn't count on that," she said when she'd finished. "Joshua told her he thought it was a stupid idea. Now she doesn't know if she even wants to be involved with this at all."

Lydia groaned. "That figures. A girl goes out with a boy and all of a sudden she's letting him tell her what she can do and what she can't do. It happens all the time."

"Not all the time," Martha Jane objected. "*All* boys aren't like that. At least, Kevin's not. He never tries to tell me what to do. He wouldn't dare!"

"Well, I guess he's the one exception then." Lydia turned back to her typewriter. "Now, what else can I say about Zack Snyder?"

"Did somebody say 'Zack Snyder'?" Cassie danced into the room, gave a little twirl, and fell backwards onto her bed. She stared up at the ceiling and smiled dreamily. "Who told you? Daphne?"

"Who told me what?" Lydia asked.

Cassie sat up and hugged her knees. "Zack asked me to go to the dance with him tomorrow night."

Lydia and Martha Jane exchanged meaningful looks. "Isn't that kind of short notice?" Lydia asked carefully. "Asking you out today for a dance tomorrow night?"

"I don't care," Cassie said. "At least I get to go to the dance now. And you have to admit, he's cute."

"Right," said Lydia. "Cute and creepy."

"How can you say that?" Cassie demanded. "You told me yourself you hardly know him."

"Lucky for me," Lydia remarked. "Cassie, he's awful. You should have seen how he acted when I tried to interview him for the *Alternative*. He just laughed."

Cassie looked at her sister sadly. "*Everyone's* laughing, Lydia. No one wants girls on the football team."

"Since when do you know what everyone wants? It doesn't matter, anyway. Once they read our paper, they'll start taking this seriously." She turned to Martha Jane for support. "Right?"

Martha Jane was silent for a minute. Her face was flushed and her eyes were watery. "I guess. Listen, I'm not feeling so great. I better go on home."

Lydia was about to say they still had lots of work to do, but she thought better of it. Martha Jane really did look pretty awful. "Okay. Why don't you ask my mom to give you a ride?"

"She's out," Cassie said. "But Dad's downstairs. I'm sure he'll take you. C'mon, I'll go down with you."

"I'll keep working on these interviews," Lydia said. "I hope you feel better." Martha Jane nodded weakly and staggered out with Cassie.

When Cassie returned, she sat down on the edge of her bed and eyed her sister glumly. "Lydia, are you really planning to go ahead with this football thing?"

"Of course," Lydia replied, "we've just started." She looked at Cassie curiously. "Why?"

Cassie seemed distinctly uncomfortable. "It's embarrassing, that's why. Kids keep coming up to me and asking me if you're some kind of wacko."

"So what? Tell them I'm a wacko if you want."

Cassie pushed a strand of hair out of her face and grimaced. "Honestly, Lydia, this time I think maybe you *are* going wacko. You've had dumb ideas before, but this is the dumbest."

"That's *your* opinion," Lydia said shortly.

"It's *everyone's* opinion. And you're my sister. If they think you're wacko, they might start thinking I'm wacko, too." She let out a long, mournful sigh. "Personally, I think maybe Zack was right to laugh at you."

Lydia gave an exaggerated yawn and tried to look nonchalant. "Maybe he won't think it's so funny when he sees what I'm going to write about him."

Cassie's eyes narrowed. "What *are* you going to write about him?"

"I'm not sure yet," Lydia said casually. "How about something like 'Zack Snyder is a stupid, ignorant chauvinist pig with a dirty mind.'"

"Lydia!" Cassie shrieked. "You wouldn't dare!"

"Why not?"

"You can't do that to me! He's maybe going to be my boyfriend! You'll ruin everything!"

Lydia stood up and faced her, hands on her hips. "You shouldn't even be going out with him. He's a total sleaze."

Cassie jumped off the bed and stood there with her arms folded. "Since when can you tell me who I can go out with? I don't have to take orders from you."

"If I tell Mom and Dad what I know about him, they won't let you go out with him."

"You're crazy!" Cassie practically screamed.

"What's going on in here?" Daphne stood at the door, her face marked with lines of concern. Right behind her was Phoebe, looking expectant and eager. "You guys having a fight?" she asked.

Lydia and Cassie didn't even acknowledge them. "I know why you're saying all this," Cassie shouted. "You're jealous, that's why!"

"Jealous!" Lydia's tone was incredulous. "Of you and Zack Snyder? Ha!"

"You're jealous because I'm going to the dance and you're not. Just because no one ever asks you out, you want to ruin everything for me!"

"Cassie!" Daphne cried out in dismay.

It was all Lydia could do to keep from screaming right back at her. Somehow she managed to keep her voice even. "For your information, I've got more important things to think about than dates and dances."

"Like girls playing football," Cassie sneered. "Oh, yeah, Lydia—that's really important."

Lydia couldn't control herself any longer. "How would you know what's important and what's not? You're too stupid to know the difference!"

"Lydia!" Daphne moaned.

They might have stood there glaring at each other forever if the phone hadn't rung. Phoebe's eyes darted back and forth from her sisters to the hallway, as if she were debating which was more interesting. Daphne gave them a beseeching look before running out into the hall to answer the phone. She reappeared a second later. "Lydia, it's for you."

Shooting one last fierce scowl at Cassie, Lydia brushed past her wide-eyed younger sisters and went out to the alcove in the hall.

"Hello?"

"Lydia, hi—this is Sam. . . ."

"Huh? Who?"

"Sam Kelsey. From school?"

It didn't take her long to recover her wits. "Oh, yeah. What do you want?"

He sounded slightly taken aback by her tone. "Well, look, I mean, I know this is last minute and all that, but I was just wondering . . ." The next words came out in a rush. "Would you like to go to the ninth-grade dance tomorrow night?"

Now it was Lydia's turn to be taken aback. "To the dance?"

"Yeah."

"With *you*?"

Sam laughed. "No, with my grandfather. Yeah, with me! How about it?"

Lydia's lips were pressed together so tightly she could barely get the next words out. "That's very funny, Sam. Very clever."

"What do you mean?" The innocence in his voice made her want to laugh out loud.

"You might think I'm a wacko, Sam, but I'm not stupid. I can see what you're trying to do."

"I'm *trying* to take you to the dance!"

"Right. Did the whole football team put you up to this?"

"What are you talking about?"

"Oh, I can just hear them all now," Lydia continued. "Take Lydia out and treat her nice and she'll be so thrilled she'll drop her campaign. Well, forget it."

"That's not true!" Sam actually had the gall to sound injured. "I wouldn't do anything like that!"

How dumb did he think she was? "Sorry, Sam. It won't work."

And before he could say another word, she hung up.

8

PHOEBE WAS SITTING at the kitchen table when Lydia came in the back door. She was eating cookies, drinking milk, and looking very contented.

"I love Fridays," she said, her mouth full. "Don't you?"

"Not *this* Friday," Lydia replied. She tossed her books on the counter, pulled a soda out of the refrigerator, and joined her sister at the table.

"What happened?" Phoebe asked.

Lydia stared into space for a moment. "I *knew* this football idea wasn't going to be as popular as the cafeteria food," she said. "But I didn't think people were going to act *this* goofy about it."

"What do you mean?"

The memory of the day's last class period flooded

her mind, and she could still feel her ears burning. "Oh, the teacher was talking about career goals and how we have to think about that when we start planning our high school programs. And this obnoxious jerk kept asking me if I was going to be a quarterback or a running back." She paused. "Everyone laughed."

"Well, whoever it was is just a creep," Phoebe said sympathetically. "And kids will laugh at anything."

"And then I went to the Student Council meeting after school. And I asked if I could get them to officially support the idea. I even made a formal motion."

"What did they say?"

"They *tabled* it. They didn't even want to discuss it. Rick Lewis said to wait until after we finished planning the Thanksgiving canned food drive and the Christmas program and the Student of the Year Award. By then, everyone will have forgotten all about it."

"Well, at least they didn't laugh," Phoebe said helpfully.

"That's not all," Lydia continued, kicking the leg of the table rhythmically. "The stupid *Cedar Century* came out today." She got up and extracted the newspaper from her pile of books. "Look."

She pointed to a crudely drawn cartoon that portrayed a group of girls in shoulder pads trying to get helmets on over their elaborate hairdos. One wore high heels with the uniform. Underneath, the caption read "The new Panthers?"

"What do you think, Fee? Pretty dumb, huh?"

Phoebe giggled, then clamped a hand over her mouth.

"Sorry. I guess they're just being silly. When is the *Alternative* coming out?"

"Who knows?" Lydia started kicking the table leg again. "Martha Jane's sick, and Emma wants to drop out. I didn't even see Kevin today. He's probably embarrassed by the whole thing. Ow!" She'd kicked too hard.

Phoebe looked alarmed. "You're not giving up, are you?"

"Of course not," Lydia replied. "It's just aggravating, that's all. On Monday kids were applauding me in class. Today, they're laughing. One minute I'm a hero and the next I'm . . . I'm a joke."

"But you can take it, right?" Phoebe gazed at her sister admiringly. "Remember when those people tried to ban the books in the public library? And when I first tried to get kids to help fight it, they laughed at me. But we talked them into it, remember? You helped me!"

"I remember."

The back door opened and Cassie breezed in. Lydia pretended not to see her. She kept her eyes focused on Phoebe and continued, in a slightly louder voice, "And I have to tell you, Fee, I really appreciate your support. It's nice to know I've got *one* sister on my side."

"I'll bet Daphne agrees with me, too," Phoebe said with conviction. "Hi, Cass."

Lydia heard a casual "Hi, Fee" behind her. She refused to turn around until footsteps assured her that Cassie had left the kitchen.

"My own sister." Lydia shook her head regretfully. "*She's* probably laughing harder than anyone else. Where's Daphne?"

"She and Mom went shopping for shoes." Phoebe paused, and cocked her head thoughtfully. "Something's going on. I saw Daphne right before she left and she was acting weird."

"How do you mean *weird*? Like spacey? That's nothing new."

"Not exactly," Phoebe said. "More like she was bummed out about something. She looked really down."

Lydia frowned. "That's strange. Maybe she's worried about a test or something."

Phoebe nodded. "I figured she's nervous about going to the dance tonight. But just a couple of days ago she was all excited."

Lydia had forgotten about the dance. She groaned. "That means Cassie will be in the bedroom for the next three hours getting ready. I better go get my typewriter and bring it down here."

She was on her way out of the room when the telephone rang.

"Hello?"

"Hi, it's Kevin."

"Hi! You want to come over and work on the *Alternative*?"

Kevin's voice was funny. "Well, uh, that's not why I'm calling. Martha Jane's got the flu. . . ."

"Yeah, that's what I figured," Lydia said. "That's going to put us behind."

"The thing is," Kevin continued, "we were supposed to go to the dance tonight."

"Well, she can't go if she's got the flu."

"I know, I know," Kevin said. "But, you see, I've already bought two tickets, and I really wanted to go." He sounded a little embarrassed. "I've never been to a dance before."

Lydia's forehead wrinkled. What was he getting at?

His next words came out rapidly. "So I was thinking maybe you'd go with me. Martha Jane said I shouldn't waste the ticket and it was okay with her and it wouldn't have to be like a real date or anything like that. . . ." His voice drifted off.

"Me? Go to the dance?" The idea was definitely not exciting. Lydia thought quickly. "Gee, I don't know, Kevin. Cassie and Daphne are going, and I think my parents are going out, and I shouldn't leave Phoebe home alone—"

"I'm spending the night at Linn's," Phoebe called out loudly. Lydia winced. She knew Kevin must have heard her.

"Oh, come on," Kevin wheedled. "If it's really awful, we can leave—I promise. I just want to see what it's like."

Lydia sighed. After all, Kevin *was* a friend. And right now, she couldn't afford to lose a friend. "Okay. What time?"

"I'll come by for you at seven-thirty," Kevin said excitedly. "Thanks!"

Lydia hung up the phone. She sat back down at the

table, plunked her elbows on the surface, and rested her chin in her hands. "What are you supposed to wear to a dance, anyway?"

"Ask Cassie," Phoebe suggested. "She's good at that kind of thing."

"No, thanks."

There was some fumbling at the back door and Lydia got up to open it. Her mother and Daphne both had their arms full with packages.

"Did you buy out the store?" Lydia asked, taking some of the bags and setting them on the table.

"There was a fabulous sale," Mrs. Gray said. "There's something for you in the green bag."

Lydia opened it and peered inside. It was a navy blue sweatshirt and matching sweatpants. "Hey, thanks, Mom."

"Did you get shoes?" Phoebe asked Daphne.

Daphne nodded and indicated a bag. While Phoebe reached inside, Lydia examined Daphne's face.

She *did* look down. Her naturally pale face was even paler, and her downcast eyes wouldn't meet Lydia's.

"These are nice," Phoebe said, pulling a pair of simple black shoes with small heels from the bag.

"Thanks," Daphne said. "I guess I better go upstairs and try them on with my dress." She didn't look particularly enthusiastic about the prospect as she took the shoes and left the kitchen. Lydia stared after her.

"What's the matter with Daphne?" she asked her mother.

Mrs. Gray looked worried, too. "I haven't the slightest idea. She barely said a word while we were out. I don't think she's sick. At least, she doesn't seem to have a fever."

"I'm going to find out what's going on," Phoebe stated with determination, taking off after her sister.

Mrs. Gray gathered up the bags. "Has your father called?"

"No," Lydia said. "Why?"

Her mother's lips twitched. "I think he's afraid to come home. He probably thinks you're lying in wait for him."

Lydia was confused. "How come?"

Her mother's mouth dropped slightly open. "Oh, dear. I guess you didn't see the paper this morning. Well, you're going to see it sooner or later." She took the morning newspaper off the counter and opened it. "Now, you know your father had nothing to do with this." She indicated the column headed "About Town."

Lydia's eyes widened as she read the brief note:

> Rumor has it the kids at Cedar Park Junior High are talking about letting girls try out for the football team. Our liberated adolescent girls are taking their pursuit of adolescent boys onto the athletic field! Not to mention the locker rooms. . . .

Lydia slumped down in her seat. "How could Dad let this jerk write this?"

"Don't be too hard on him," her mother said. "You know he tries to let his columnists write what they like."

She sat down across from her at the table. "I know, it's a bad joke. But it's just one person's opinion. Don't let it get you down. And please don't kick the table leg."

Lydia hadn't even realized she'd started doing that again. "Mom, do you think this is a dumb idea?"

"Nope," her mother said promptly. "In fact, I can't wait to tell my women's group about it Sunday."

Great, Lydia thought. At least they won't laugh. On the other hand, they won't be able to help much either. Suddenly, she didn't feel much like talking about it. She got up and took the green bag off the table. "I'll take this upstairs," she said. "I really like it, Mom." She paused on her way out of the kitchen. "By the way, I'm going to the dance tonight."

She couldn't help but enjoy her mother's stunned look and momentary speechlessness.

"You're going to the dance?"

"Yeah. Martha Jane's sick, and Kevin doesn't want to waste the ticket."

Mrs. Gray smiled. "Well, this will be a new experience for you. What are you going to wear?"

Lydia raised her hands in a helpless gesture. As she walked upstairs, she wondered briefly whether she could get away with wearing her new sweats. She had a pretty good suspicion they wouldn't be exactly appropriate.

She had just finished putting the sweats away in her drawer when Phoebe hurried in, closing the door behind her.

"What are you doing that for?" Lydia asked.

Phoebe spoke in a whisper. "Where's Cassie?"

"Taking a bath, I guess. What's going on?"

Phoebe sat on the bed and wrapped her arms around her knees. "Daphne would kill me if she knew I was telling you this. She told me not to tell anyone."

Lydia looked at her in bewilderment. "Tell me what?"

"Why she's so down."

Lydia sat on the other bed. "Why won't she tell me herself? Is it something I did?"

"Sort of," Phoebe said, biting her lip.

Lydia remembered a time, just a month ago, when she'd signed Daphne up to run for class office without asking her. It had taken Daphne ages before she got up the nerve to tell Lydia she didn't want to do it. But Lydia hadn't tried to push her around lately.

"Okay, tell me. What did I do to her this time?"

"It's not exactly anything you did *to* her," Phoebe said hesitantly.

"Fee! Tell me!"

"Shhh." Phoebe glanced furtively at the closed door. "See, some of the kids at school have been teasing her. Because of your football thing."

"You're kidding!" Lydia was honestly shocked. "Why would they tease *her*?"

"Because she's your sister, dummy! Cassie said she was getting hassled too, remember?"

Lydia dismissed that. "Cassie's always complaining about everything I do. She can handle it."

"But Daphne's different," Phoebe noted. "You know how she is."

Lydia fell silent. Phoebe was right—Daphne *was* different. She didn't like too much attention, not even the positive kind. And if kids were really picking on her, she must be miserable.

"They're really giving her a lot of grief?" she asked Phoebe.

Phoebe's head bobbed. "Just the same kind of jokes you were telling me about. And Daphne tried to defend you. But she got really upset, and you can guess what happened then."

Lydia nodded slowly. "She started crying."

"Right. So now she's really embarrassed about seeing those boys again."

"Oh, no," Lydia sighed. "Why didn't she come and tell me about this?"

Phoebe shrugged. "I don't know. I guess she doesn't want to make you feel bad."

Lydia got up and paced the room. She was about to ask what Phoebe thought she should do, when she realized she'd be seeking advice from a sixth grader.

"She'll get over it," Phoebe said wisely. "And there's nothing you can do about it. I gotta get over to Linn's." She got up to leave, and paused at the door. "Don't tell anyone I told you about this, okay? Promise?"

"I won't. I promise."

After Phoebe left, Lydia stopped pacing and threw herself back on her bed. Now what was she going to do? First, there were the kids laughing at her in school. Then the dumb *Century* cartoon and that stupid remark in her father's newspaper. And now Daphne.

Poor Daphne. She was so sensitive. How could Lydia

subject her to ridicule? How could she make her suffer like this? What kind of sister was she, anyway?

Finally, she got off the bed and went to her closet. She scanned the contents, looking for something to wear to the dance. But as she flipped through the clothes, she felt more and more depressed.

And it wasn't just because of the dance.

9

LYDIA STOOD AT THE ENTRANCE to the gym, slipped off her coat, and adjusted the collar of the beaded sweater she had borrowed from her mother.

"The place looks great," Kevin said enthusiastically.

Lydia had to admit it looked a lot more festive than usual. Bright paper streamers fell from the ceiling, along with clusters of balloons. The kids looked different, too. Some of them had gotten really dressed up. Over in one corner was a man surrounded by a lot of fancy equipment playing records.

Lydia felt positively formal in her black skirt. She hadn't worn a skirt in ages, and she wasn't exactly comfortable. She thought she probably looked okay. Cassie had pretty much monopolized the space in front of the mirror in their bedroom. Somehow they'd managed to get dressed in the same room without exchanging one word.

"Let's check out the refreshments," Kevin suggested. They wandered over to a long table set up at one end of the gym. Lydia waved to a few friends who looked more than a little surprised to see her there. She spotted Daphne and Rick Lewis in front of the punch bowl, and she and Kevin joined them.

"Hi, guys," she said, surveying the various goodies on the table. Rick whistled.

"Wow, Lydia, I almost didn't recognize you. You look terrific."

Lydia could feel her face go warm. "Uh, yeah, thanks." Self-consciously, she touched her hair, as if to assure herself it was the same hair she wore with her jeans.

She scrutinized her sister. Daphne greeted her too, but she looked a little uneasy, and she kept glancing apprehensively at the dance floor. Lydia felt an enormous urge to reassure her, to tell her she wouldn't get hassled anymore. But she remembered her promise to Phoebe and could only offer Daphne a hearty smile.

Daphne smiled back, if a little weakly. "This is nice," she said, gesturing toward the decorations. Lydia nodded in agreement. Her little sister's first big dance! Of course, she shouldn't feel too superior. It was *her* first dance, too.

Kevin was rapidly chewing on a miniature sandwich. "You want to dance?" he asked.

"Uh, let me get something to eat first," Lydia said quickly. She grabbed a sandwich and began taking tiny bites, trying to make it last as long as possible.

"I was thinking," Rick said, "about that idea you brought up at Student Council today—"

Out of the corner of her eye, Lydia could see Daphne flinch.

"Oh, let's not talk about that now," Lydia interrupted. "I'm getting sick of it."

Rick raised his eyebrows. "That doesn't sound like you."

Lydia popped the rest of the sandwich in her mouth and turned to Kevin. "Let's dance." It was either that or listen to another lecture on why girls couldn't play football and watch her sister shrivel with embarrassment. She figured dancing would be the lesser of two unpleasant experiences.

Luckily, the area reserved for dancing was fairly crowded and Lydia could pretty much stand still and just bring her arms up and down in rhythm to the music. Kevin, on the other hand, wanted to *dance*. He was actually moving both his arms and his legs—and looking pretty good.

"Where'd you learn to do that?" Lydia asked.

"I got this video and I've been practicing at home," Kevin said breathlessly.

No wonder he was so intent on going to the dance. Lydia glanced around uneasily. Sure enough, a few people were actually watching them. Among them was Sam Kelsey. When their eyes met, he grinned. Lydia looked away.

"Let's move," she told Kevin urgently.

"Sure! Watch this!" He began doing some intricate side step. In agony, Lydia tried to keep up with him.

They ended up back toward the entrance to the gym. It wasn't a better position. Now Lydia had a clear view of Cassie and Zack Snyder, standing just inside the entrance.

They weren't dancing. Lydia couldn't hear what they were saying, but Cassie's expression was a very familiar one. Her sister was angry.

"Do that step again," she instructed Kevin. Kevin was happy to oblige. He moved toward the other side of the gym and Lydia managed to follow him. When they were finally situated in one spot, she went back to her automatic arm jerking and let her mind wander.

She wondered what was going on between Cassie and Zack. Maybe he'd done something outrageous. He'd probably flirted with another girl—he seemed like the type. Or maybe he'd tried something with Cassie. He had that kind of reputation.

You shouldn't care, Lydia told herself firmly. *If she's dumb enough to go out with him, she deserves what she gets.*

"Hey, Lydia!" She glanced up. A couple of guys from the football team were standing on the edge of the dance area. One of them held a paper cup in his hand. "Catch!" He held his arm back like he was about to make a forward pass and threw the cup as if it was a football. It landed on the floor, next to Lydia's feet. Without missing a beat, she neatly crumpled it with her foot.

"Knock it off, you guys."

She looked up again. It was Sam Kelsey. Great—now he was defending her. What kind of game was he playing, anyway?

"Kevin, I'm beat. Why don't you just stay here and

keep dancing? I'm going to get something to drink."

Kevin nodded happily, his head bouncing in rhythm to the music. As she made her way off the dance floor, she saw Zack again—but not with Cassie. He was leading some other girl onto the floor.

At the refreshment table, she encountered Cassie's friend, Barbie. "Have you seen Cassie around?" she asked, trying to sound unconcerned.

"I think she's in the rest room," Barbie replied. "She had a fight with Zack."

"A fight? What were they fighting about?"

Barbie looked a little uncomfortable. "I think they were fighting about you."

"About me?"

"Barbie, let's dance." Some boy grabbed her hand, and with an apologetic smile to Lydia, Barbie allowed herself to be pulled away. Lydia walked through the crowd, out the entrance, and across the hall to the rest room.

Cassie was standing in front of a mirror, slowly dragging a comb through her hair. When she saw Lydia's reflection in the mirror, she faltered, her comb suspended in midair. She didn't speak—but at least she didn't look away.

Lydia hopped up and perched on the edge of a sink. She mentally pushed all hostilities aside and got directly to the point. "What happened between you and Zack?"

Apparently, Cassie wasn't quite ready to call a truce. Silently, she put her comb back in her purse, withdrew a lip liner, and began carefully outlining her lips.

"C'mon, Cass. What happened?"

Cassie wasn't about to be rushed. Lydia waited while

Cassie finished lining her lips. She had to apply her lipstick and her gloss before she got around to responding. "We had a fight."

She pulled a tissue from a dispenser and blotted her lips carefully. When she didn't volunteer any additional information, Lydia spoke again.

"What were you fighting about?"

Cassie tossed the makeup back in her purse and finally faced Lydia. "Okay, okay—you were right, I was wrong. Are you happy now?"

Lydia threw up her hands in bewilderment. Doing so, she lost her balance on the edge of the sink. She grabbed wildly for the faucet, but it wasn't much help. She landed in the bowl.

Cassie's mouth fell open. "Lydia, get out of there before someone comes in and sees you!"

Lydia waved her arms helplessly in the air. Cassie clutched them and pulled her out of the sink. With her feet planted safely on the floor, she had a mental picture of the way she must have looked in the sink, and burst out laughing. Cassie started laughing, too.

"You've got wet spots all over that skirt," Cassie pointed out, still giggling.

Lydia flapped her skirt in the air. "It'll dry. What did you mean, I was right? I know I usually *am*, but what exactly are you talking about?"

Cassie stopped giggling. She folded her arms and leaned against the wall. "Zack. You were right about him. How can someone so cute be such a creep?"

It took every ounce of Lydia's willpower to keep from shrieking "I told you so." "What did he do?"

"Oh, he didn't actually *do* anything. Just things he was saying . . ." Her voice drifted off and she turned back to the mirror.

"Like what?" Lydia persisted.

Reluctantly, Cassie faced her. "Dumb stuff. About you. He kept making all these stupid jokes about your football idea. He said you wanted to play on the football team because it would be the only way you'd ever get a guy to touch you."

"Is he crazy?" Lydia asked in disgust. "I don't even *want* to play football. It's the principle of the thing."

"I know that," Cassie said. "He's just got a dirty mind."

Lydia looked at her curiously. "What did *you* say?"

Cassie's lips twisted into something halfway between a smile and a grimace. "I told him he didn't understand. Then he called you a wacko, and I said he couldn't talk about my sister like that. Then he said he'd talk any way he wanted to and if I didn't like it, that was too bad. So I said 'Too bad for *you*' and walked away."

Lydia was stunned. "You—you defended me?"

Cassie nodded.

"But *you* were the one who kept calling me a wacko."

"Oh, I still think you're crazy," Cassie said hastily. "But I'm your sister. It's okay for me to call you wacko. I just can't let somebody else get away with that." A mournful look crossed her face. "Even someone as cute as Zack."

"I don't get it," Lydia said. "I *told* you he laughed at me. And you said he was right!"

Cassie made a face. "It didn't sound so bad, the way

92

you described it. But when he did it right in front of me, I couldn't help it. I got mad!"

Lydia was silent for a second. Then she smiled. "Wow, Cassie. You were really being loyal. That's nice."

"Well, you *are* my sister. Even if you're nuts."

Lydia's smile widened. "I guess you're not so stupid after all."

"Gee, thanks."

Lydia stopped smiling. "Really, Cass—I mean it. I know it wasn't easy for you to say that to Zack. And I really appreciate your sticking up for me."

"It's okay," Cassie mumbled, looking away.

Lydia turned to glance at her own reflection. She thought she looked tired. "I don't know, Cass. Maybe *you're* right. Maybe it *is* a dumb idea. Girls playing football . . . I'm getting nothing but grief."

"Why don't you get back into your nuclear disarmament thing?" Cassie asked. "At least there are people who will agree with you."

"Yeah. Listen, you want to hang around here? I don't mean the rest room, I mean the dance."

"Not particularly. I don't even want to see that jerk Zack."

"Let's find Kevin and go home."

They left the rest room and went back across the hall to the gym. Lydia's eyes scanned the room. A small crowd had gathered in one corner.

Cassie pointed toward them. "There's Kevin."

Lydia squinted. "What's he doing?"

"I think he's trying to breakdance."

"Oh, yeah—now I see him." She watched for a

moment. "He's having a really good time. I hate to ask him to leave."

"We're not supposed to walk home alone after dark," Cassie reminded her. "Dad would kill us."

"I know." Lydia turned to her. "Don't you think that's sexist?"

"Sexist?"

"They say we're not supposed to walk home after dark, even if it's the two of us together. But if any wimpy guy walks with us, it's okay. It doesn't make sense."

Cassie considered this. "You know, for once I think you might be right. If I was a mugger, I'd be more scared of you than Kevin."

"Why?"

"You look meaner. And tougher."

"Thanks," Lydia said automatically. They both started giggling. It didn't last long, though—Cassie stopped when Zack ambled past them, his arm loosely draped around some girl.

Cassie stared after them. "I really want to get out of here."

"I know," Lydia said sympathetically. Maybe Zack was a total creep, but Cassie was still hurting. "I guess we could ask Rick and Daphne to walk with us."

"That's not fair," Cassie objected. "It's her first dance." Her eyes seemed to focus on something. "Wait a minute."

She ran back toward the gym entrance. Sam Kelsey was standing there, putting on his football jacket. Lydia groaned silently as she watched Cassie have a brief

94

conversation with him. Then she beckoned to Lydia.

Lydia tried to send her a message with her eyes, but Cassie just kept waving her over. Unwillingly, Lydia joined them.

"Sam's leaving and he says he'll walk us home."

"Great," Lydia muttered.

Her tone didn't appear to bother Sam at all. "No problem," he said. He waited for them to get their coats, held the door for them, and followed them out.

"He's so polite," Cassie whispered. Lydia shrugged.

They walked along in silence for a minute. It was beginning to feel awkward, and Lydia tried to think of something bland to say. "It's cold."

"Sure is," Sam said.

He was probably going to agree with everything she said.

"Did you come alone?" Cassie asked him.

Sam nodded. "How about you?"

Cassie sniffed. "I came with Zack Snyder. Is he a good friend of yours?"

"No," Sam replied. "We just play football together."

"Well, he's a creep," Cassie proclaimed decisively. To Lydia's horror, she went on to tell him what had happened at the dance.

"He said that?" Sam turned to Lydia. "That's terrible."

Lydia had to admit Sam was a terrific actor. He actually sounded shocked.

"About this coed football thing," he said slowly, "I think that—"

"I really don't want to know what you think," Lydia snapped.

"Lydia!" Cassie pursed her lips disapprovingly.

Lydia sighed. After all, the guy *was* walking them home, probably out of his way. "Sorry. I guess I just don't feel like talking about it."

"Yeah, I guess some kids have been giving you a pretty rough time. But that newspaper of yours is a great idea. We need something like that."

"Thanks," Lydia said shortly.

"Lydia's always got a cause," Cassie informed him.

"Yeah, I can tell. You stand up for things."

Lydia felt like she had to say something. "I think you have to fight for what you believe in." She paused. "As long as it's something worth believing in."

"How do you know what's worth believing in?" Sam asked her.

"You just know," Lydia said simply.

Cassie jumped in. "Our dad says Lydia's a born leader. He thinks she's going to be a great lawyer and fight injustice."

Lydia glanced at her sideways through narrowed eyes. What was she up to? She looked to her other side to see how Sam was reacting. He looked cheerful.

"You're pretty tough, aren't you?"

Lydia didn't know how to respond to that. She shrugged, smiled briefly, and made a noncommittal gesture that was more or less a yes.

Sam nodded in approval. "That's cool."

10

E ARLY MONDAY MORNING, Lydia sat at the
foot of her bed, tying the laces on her sneakers. In the
other bed, Cassie stirred, opened her eyes slightly, and
raised herself up on one elbow.

"You want to borrow my pink sweater?" Cassie's voice
was thick with sleep.

"No, thanks," Lydia replied. "Why would I want to
borrow your pink sweater?"

Cassie sank back on her pillow. "Because it would
look good with your coloring. And you might run into
Sam Kelsey."

"I don't get the connection," Lydia lied.

Cassie gave an exasperated groan and hoisted herself
up again. "He *likes* you, dummy. And I'll bet he'd like

you even better in pink. Guys like girls to wear pastel colors."

Lydia got up. Her gray pullover, which had once belonged to her father and had shrunk in the wash, felt soft and warm and comforting. And she needed all the comfort she could get today.

"I hate pastel colors. And I'm not about to change the way I dress for some boy. Especially some dumb jock."

"I don't think he's a dumb jock," Cassie argued. "He's cute. And he's nice, too. He didn't even say anything nasty about your football idea."

Lydia went over to the mirror and pulled a comb quickly through her hair. "And that's supposed to make me fall madly in love with him? Just because he didn't say anything nasty?"

Cassie fell back again. "Lydia, you're hopeless. C'mon, tell the truth. Don't you like him just a teeny little bit?"

Lydia grabbed her backpack and slung it over her shoulder. "I'll see you at school." She ran downstairs and into the kitchen.

Her mother was stirring something in a pot on the stove. "Another early *Alternative* meeting?" she asked Lydia.

"Yep." Lydia reached in the refrigerator for the carton of orange juice. She was just about to take a swig when she remembered her mother was standing there. She took a glass from the dish drain.

"How about some oatmeal?" her mother asked.

"No, thanks. I told Martha Jane and Kevin eight o'clock, and I don't want to be late."

"I'm looking forward to seeing this issue," Mrs. Gray said. "You know, I told my women's group what you kids were up to. And they were *very* intrigued. In fact, you might be interested to know that one woman—"

"Wait a minute," Lydia interrupted. "Before you get too excited, I better tell you—I don't know if we're going to be doing the issue on football. Not this week." She didn't add "maybe never."

She turned slightly so she wouldn't have to see her mother's expression. It didn't help. She could hear the surprise in her voice.

"Why not? It's such a good idea!"

Lydia paused for a quick mental debate. She couldn't tell her mother about the kids bothering Daphne—she'd promised. But giving up wasn't her style, and her mother knew that.

"I don't know," she said casually. "It's just getting kind of boring. And no one at school seems very up for it."

"But you knew it wouldn't be a very popular cause."

Lydia took half an English muffin and began chewing hard so she wouldn't have to answer. It wasn't toasted, but she didn't care.

"Besides," Mrs. Gray continued, "I thought you felt so strongly about it. This doesn't sound like you, Lydia. Are you really going to let a little opposition change your mind?"

Lydia swallowed. "It's not that," she said quickly. "I guess it's just not all that important."

Her mother looked at her doubtfully. "It was pretty important just a couple of days ago."

Lydia picked up her backpack. "I've gotta run." She started out of the kitchen, but not fast enough to miss her mother's parting words.

"Well, if you can't take the heat, I guess you'd better get out of the kitchen."

Lydia pretended not to hear. She went to the hall closet and got her coat. As she was pulling it on, her father came down the stairs.

"Good morning," he said cheerfully. "You must be feeling vindicated."

"What do you mean?" Lydia asked.

Her father smiled widely. "Guess you haven't seen the morning paper. Take a look when you get to school."

Probably something about the new food service at school, Lydia thought as she walked quickly toward school. The weather had turned suddenly colder, and the biting wind almost penetrated her coat. Well, at least the *Alternative* had accomplished *something*. Now, if only they could come up with another idea the kids would support. Something different, something important, something . . . something the kids wouldn't laugh at. Something that wouldn't bother her shy little sister.

When Lydia got to school, the halls were empty. She stopped by her locker first to get rid of her coat. Then she headed for the school library.

Martha Jane and Kevin were waiting at a table. Luckily, no one else was around. Even the librarian was in her back office. Lydia was relieved. She really didn't want anyone else to hear what she was about to say. She wasn't accustomed to admitting defeat, and she certainly didn't want to do it in public.

I'm doing this for Daphne, she told herself, thinking it would make her feel noble and self-sacrificing. It didn't.

"Hi," she said briefly, and before either of her friends could reply, she went directly into the speech she'd been going over and over in her head. She took a deep breath.

"I think we should come up with a different topic for the *Alternative.* This idea of letting girls try out for football is turning into a big joke. If we devote the entire issue of the *Alternative* to it, the newspaper's going to turn into a big joke and nobody's going to take us seriously anymore. I know it was my idea to start this campaign, but it was a bad idea, I admit it. I was wrong and I apologize."

She let out what little breath she had left. She felt drained. That had to be the most difficult speech she'd ever made. She hated to be wrong. Even more than that, she hated to admit it.

Kevin and Martha Jane exchanged glances. "I don't think it was such a bad idea," Kevin said. Lydia gave him a small smile. It was sweet of him to try to make her feel better.

Martha Jane agreed with him. "When I was sick this weekend, a couple of kids called to see how I was feeling. And we got to talking about this. They both ended up saying they thought it was a kind of neat idea."

Lydia brushed that aside. "Big deal. Two kids."

"If there are two who feel that way," Kevin noted, "there're probably more. We just haven't heard from them."

"They're too busy laughing at us," Lydia said.

Martha Jane eyed her curiously. "You know who you sound like?"

"Who?"

"Cassie. You sound just like Cassie."

Lydia sat down and glared at Martha Jane. "What's *that* supposed to mean?"

"You know what I mean," Martha Jane replied. "Worried about what everyone thinks of you, that sort of thing. I thought you didn't care about being popular."

"Don't be ridiculous," Lydia snapped. "I don't care what people say about me."

"Oh, yeah? Then how come you want to give up?"

Lydia put her elbows on the table and rested her chin in her hands. "Because it's a waste of time. Because if we don't have any support at all, what's the point in going on?"

"What did you think of those letters in your father's paper?" Martha Jane asked.

"What letters?"

Kevin went over to the newspaper rack and returned with that morning's copy of the *Cedar Park Journal*. He opened it to the editorial page and handed it to Lydia. "Take a look."

There were three letters to the editor.

" 'I was appalled by the joking reference to the plan on the part of enlightened junior high students to allow girls the opportunity to play football,' " Lydia read. " 'You owe them all an apology.' "

Another letter began, "The Panthers need all the help they can get. If the girls want to play football, let them."

And the third referred to the columnist as "a male chauvinist pig who doesn't know what he's talking about."

Lydia's eyes widened as she read. "This is amazing. They *like* the idea."

"See, I told you we had support," Kevin remarked.

Lydia put the newspaper down. "Yeah, but these people aren't students at Cedar Park Junior High. And that's where the support has to come from."

"I just know kids will get excited once they know what we're really talking about," Martha Jane persisted. "And they'll never know unless we put out the newspaper."

Lydia groaned. She was going to have to break her promise. "It's not just getting the support," she said. "And you know *I* don't care if people laugh at us. But there's something else. Daphne's been getting teased a lot about this, really hassled. And you know how she is. . . ."

"Scared of her own shadow," Martha Jane said promptly.

Lydia grimaced. "She's not *that* bad. She's just sensitive, that's all. She gets really upset if people laugh at her."

"Not like you," Martha Jane murmured.

Lydia looked at her suspiciously. Was there a note of sarcasm in her voice?

"Hi, everyone" came a voice behind her. Lydia turned to see Emma, clutching a notebook.

"Hi," Martha Jane and Kevin said together. Lydia wasn't quite so friendly. After all, Emma had been the rat who had jumped the sinking ship—the minute her boyfriend had expressed displeasure with the *Alternative's* topic, she'd cut out. Lydia gave her only the most fleeting of smiles.

Emma joined them at the table. "How's the issue going?"

"Not so great," Lydia said curtly. "It looks like we have to find another subject to deal with."

Emma actually looked dismayed. "But I've done all this work!" She opened her notebook, pulled out two neatly typed pages, and handed them to Lydia.

Lydia scanned them. It was an essay about the first women athletes who played sports that had previously only been played by men. Emma even had a paragraph about women wrestlers.

"This is pretty good," Lydia murmured as she read. Then she remembered who she was talking to, and glowered. "I thought you weren't going to work on this issue because Joshua thought it was dumb."

Emma had the courtesy to look sheepish. "I wasn't going to, because I was afraid he wouldn't like me any more. But then I thought about it. I decided I shouldn't let him tell me what to do. And if he really likes me, it shouldn't make any difference."

"And if it does," Martha Jane interjected, "you wouldn't want him for a boyfriend."

"I guess that's right," Emma admitted.

Kevin had taken the pages from Lydia, and he was reading them. "This is a nice article," he said. "It would be a shame to waste it."

"We shouldn't give up," Martha Jane urged. "If we

got to work right after school, we could probably whip up a whole issue by tonight. We've already got Emma's article here ready to go."

"And my cousin's photocopy shop is open till ten," Kevin added, looking excited. "The minute we finish, I could take it over there. We could have the *Alternative* ready to hand out tomorrow morning."

"Maybe," Lydia said reluctantly. She had a vision of herself handing out the *Alternative* and watching kids double over laughing, using the newspaper to make paper airplanes, cracking jokes about helmets and shoulder pads. And there was Daphne to think of. . . .

But then she studied the faces at the table, all looking up at her expectantly. What could she say? "Okay. We'll meet at my place right after school."

"Great!" Kevin said with exuberance, and the others agreed happily. Lydia wished she could share their enthusiasm. She forced a grin, mumbled something about getting to her locker, and left them.

Now the halls were filled with kids heading for homerooms. Lydia was barely aware of them. Something was bugging her. Something Martha Jane had said. . . .

Was it really because of Daphne that she wanted to dump the whole project? Was she using her sister as an excuse, a cop-out? And there was another question, one that caused a sinking sensation in the pit of her stomach.

Was she being like Cassie? Not that she didn't love her sister, and even admire her in some ways. But she'd always made fun of the way Cassie would do anything for popularity, the way she worried about seeming "different." For the first time, Lydia understood how Cassie felt.

The thought horrified her. She, Lydia Gray, school rebel and leader, was afraid of people laughing at her. The idea was so shocking she stopped walking suddenly. A boy behind her collided into her.

"Excuse me," Lydia said automatically.

The boy grinned. "You'll never make a touchdown if you stop moving in the middle of the field."

Lydia didn't bother responding. Her thoughts were all jumbled and confused. So she'd figured something out about herself. Now what?

Well, she actually did have to go to her locker for a book. When she got there, she noticed that a folded piece of paper had been squeezed halfway into the opening.

She pulled it out and opened it. She didn't recognize the handwriting.

"Good luck on your campaign to let girls go out for football. No matter what you think, there are a lot of kids here at school who support you. Give people a chance to think about this and they'll come around. Most kids aren't as quick to take a stand as you are, but don't give up. Believe it or not, lots of kids admire you."

There was no name at the bottom. It was signed "Your biggest admirer."

Lydia read it through twice. Maybe Martha Jane or Kevin had written it to make her think there *were* some kids behind them. But when could they have put it in her locker? It hadn't been there when she'd arrived at school, and she'd been with Martha Jane and Kevin ever since. Emma, maybe? But Emma didn't even know she'd been feeling discouraged.

She took a closer look at the handwriting. It was large, bold, and sprawling. And she didn't have the slightest idea whose it could be.

It didn't matter. Somebody believed in her mission. And, according to this letter, there were more like him or her. A tingle shot through her, like a small fire that had died out for a while and had suddenly sprung to life.

Let them laugh! Who cared? She had a campaign to lead. And there would be followers. This was an idea whose time had come!

And Daphne wasn't a baby. She'd have to learn not to let other kids bother her. Lydia couldn't shelter her from everything. Daphne probably wouldn't even want her to.

Lydia carefully refolded the note and stuck it in her backpack. She extracted the book she needed from the locker, and slammed the door shut. Then, head high, she marched down the hall toward her homeroom.

Give up? Never!

11

LYDIA STOOD in front of the school entrance, clutching the stack of *Alternatives* and shivering. She couldn't tell if it was from the cold or the excitement.

"Here's the cup for the money," Emma said. "Where should I put the poster?"

"We're not supposed to stick anything on the door without permission," Lydia told her. "How about leaning it on the ledge? Everyone should be able to see it there."

She watched while Emma carefully placed it in position. It didn't look bad, considering they had frantically made the posters late the night before after finishing the *Alternative*. It was a simple announcement, straightforward and to the point: "Coed Football—Yes or No? Come to a meeting on Thursday at four and talk about it."

Emma stepped back and looked at the poster. "Something's wrong."

Lydia squinted. "There's no place! We didn't say where the meeting is!"

"Where *is* the meeting going to be?" Emma asked.

Lydia clapped a hand to her head. "We didn't even think about that! I'll go to the principal's office right now and see if we can get a room here at school." She ran into the almost deserted school and up the stairs to the office.

"I need to reserve a room for a meeting on Thursday afternoon," she told the secretary.

The secretary peered at her through narrowed eyes. "What *kind* of a meeting?"

Lydia really didn't want to have to go into a full explanation. "It's for the *Alternative*—you know, the newspaper?"

The secretary's expression clearly told her that she didn't know.

"We need a big room," Lydia continued rapidly, "because it's an open meeting. How about the one on the third floor that the Student Council uses?"

"Is this an official school-sponsored organization?" the secretary asked.

Lydia bit her lower lip. "Um, not exactly. . . ."

Just then, Mr. Fletcher emerged from his office. "Well, good morning, Lydia," he said jovially. "What sort of revolution are you stirring up today?"

Lydia thrust a copy of the *Alternative* at him. "See for yourself!"

Mr. Fletcher looked at the front page. He read silently

for a minute, and then his eyebrows shot up. "Girls on the football team?"

Lydia sighed. How many times had she heard *that* in the past week? But she forced herself to be polite. "We think it's something worth discussing," she said carefully. "Equal opportunity and all that. Don't you think girls should have the same rights as boys?"

"Of course," Mr. Fletcher said, frowning slightly. "But—football?"

"We want to have a meeting Thursday afternoon to discuss it," Lydia continued. "Is it okay if we reserve the big classroom on the third floor?"

Mr. Fletcher's tone was wary. "I suppose so."

"And you'll be there? And bring Coach Benson too, okay?"

Still looking a little befuddled, Mr. Fletcher nodded. Quickly, Lydia made the arrangements with the secretary, then ran back outside to join Emma.

Kids were starting to arrive, and Emma was surrounded. Lydia got a felt-tip pen from her pack and added the room information to the poster.

"How come you got such a big room?" came a voice from behind her. Lydia turned to see Zack Snyder standing there with an insolent grin on his face. She snapped the top back on her pen and tossed it in her pack. Maybe if she didn't respond he'd go away. He didn't.

"I mean, you could probably fit everyone who comes into a closet," he added.

"I doubt it," Lydia said coolly. "I don't think Mr. Fletcher and Coach Benson will want to meet in a closet."

Zack was taken aback. "The coach is coming?"

Actually, Lydia couldn't guarantee that. So she simply flashed Zack a "so there!" look and turned to a group of kids coming up the steps.

"Get your *Alternative!* Only ten cents! Find out why girls can play football!"

The papers practically flew out of her hands. There were a few of the usual jokes, but this time they didn't bother her. There were a lot of other comments, too.

Two friends of Cassie's, Alison and Dana, huddled over a copy. "I used to throw a football around with my brothers," Alison was saying. "They always told me I'd be a great wide receiver."

"I wouldn't mind wearing one of those uniforms," Dana added. "Padded shoulders make your waist look smaller."

"Look!" Emma hissed to Lydia. "They're copying the poster!" Sure enough, several kids had paused to read it and were busily writing down the time and place.

Luckily, they'd had enough money to run off more issues this time. Even so, they sold out before the bell.

"What did Joshua say when you told him you were going to work on this?" Lydia asked Emma as they gathered up their stuff and headed into school.

Emma giggled. "First he tried to talk me out of it. When he realized he couldn't, he spent about two hours explaining all the rules of football to me."

"That's neat!" Lydia exclaimed. "Maybe this is really going to catch on!"

The practical side of Emma came out. "It's one thing

to convince the students. We'll still have to get the administration on our side."

"Well, that's what our meeting's for," Lydia replied. "See ya later!" She hurried to her homeroom, getting there a few seconds before the bell.

She took her seat and noticed with pleasure that the two boys in front of her were reading the *Alternative*. One of them looked around the classroom, punched his friend's shoulder, and indicated a girl who had just walked in.

"Running back," he said.

The other guy studied the girl in question, and shook his head. "Tight end."

Lydia glared at them suspiciously, waiting for the punch line. To her amazement and delight, none came. They both looked perfectly serious.

The kids were drifting in slowly. Some came in groups, others alone. Their expressions ranged from mild curiosity to keen enthusiasm to downright discomfort. The last group kept glancing around apprehensively, as if they were afraid someone might see them there.

Lydia couldn't even identify her own feelings. Looking at her colleagues, she suspected they were experiencing the same combination of emotions. Emma had her hands clenched so tightly her knuckles were white. Martha Jane was flushed and her lips were quivering. Kevin was maintaining some semblance of cool, but the way his eyes kept darting around the room betrayed him.

Already, the room was almost half-full, and people were still coming in. "I didn't think there'd be this many people," Emma whispered to Lydia. "I hope they're not going to start booing or anything like that."

"They won't," Lydia assured her, but her tone carried more confidence than she felt. True, she hadn't heard as many wisecracks since the *Alternative* had come out. But she still didn't know how much support they had.

She saw Cassie standing at the door, peering in. When she spotted Alison and a couple of her other Pep Club friends, she looked relieved and joined them. A second later, Daphne came in, took a seat toward the back, and gave a little tentative wave to Lydia.

"Uh-oh," Martha Jane murmured, "here comes the football team." Lydia watched as four players strolled in, looking a little self-conscious. But walking with them, Sam Kelsey didn't seem uneasy at all. In fact, he came right up to the table where the *Alternative* staff was sitting.

"Good luck," he said to Lydia.

His smile was so infectious, she couldn't resist grinning back. "Thanks," she murmured.

She watched as he took a seat alongside the other players. She turned to Kevin with a pleased expression. It faded quickly when she noticed he looked disturbed.

"What's the matter?" she asked.

"Those football players," he said. "I hope they're not planning to disrupt the meeting."

"Sam wouldn't let them do that," she said automatically, and then stopped, surprised at her own response. Did she really believe that?

The room was actually filling up. And they weren't all students—several teachers had arrived. Mr. Fletcher had come in, followed by a reluctant-looking Coach Benson. And there was her mother, with Phoebe and some other woman who looked vaguely familiar.

"Lydia!" Martha Jane exclaimed. "That's the mayor!"

Lydia's mouth dropped open. Her mother had mentioned something about bringing a woman from her group. She hadn't bothered to tell her it was the mayor— probably because she knew it would only make Lydia more nervous.

Would it be possible to feel any more nervous than she was feeling right that minute? She discovered the answer to that when a young man carrying a camera approached their table.

"*Cedar Park Journal*," he said crisply, by way of introduction. "Mind if I get a shot of you kids?"

Her father hadn't even told her the paper would be covering the meeting! She managed what she imagined to be a sickly grin as the man took some photos and then retreated to a corner of the room where he took up a notebook, looking at them expectantly.

Lydia stood up and faced the room. Thank goodness she'd written down her opening remarks on notecards. She looked out over the audience, caught her mother's supportive smile, and began.

"Good afternoon, and thank you for coming to this meeting. We're here to discuss the possibility of allowing Cedar Park Junior High girls to try out for the football team. We, the staff members of the *Alternative*, believe that all school activities should be open to both girls and boys. We think it's a question of equal opportunity. Not letting the girls go out for football is denying them their rights to full and equal participation in extracurricular activities."

She paused to take a breath, and the room started humming. Everyone seemed to be talking at once. "Hey!" Lydia shouted, "I haven't finished!" Then she gulped. What if the mayor was one of the people talking?

"Right now I'm going to introduce the members of the *Alternative* staff. Each one will make a statement. Then we'll open the floor to discussion."

She introduced Kevin first, who talked about how the Athletic Department actually discriminated against girls. Then Emma discussed the fact that many girls had the physical qualifications to play football.

Lydia had just introduced Martha Jane when Zack Snyder jumped up. Lydia's heart sank. She hadn't even seen him come in.

"Since when are we going to let four radicals tell us how to run our school?" he yelled. "As cocaptain of the Panthers, I've gotta say this is the dumbest idea I've ever heard!"

Before Lydia could say anything, the room started buzzing again. Sam Kelsey got up and gave Zack a fierce look. "As the other cocaptain of the Panthers, *I've* gotta say shut up and let them speak!"

Lydia recovered her wits. "Thank you. And it's not just four radicals supporting this idea. Go ahead, Martha Jane."

Martha Jane's voice was a little shaky, but she got the message across. "For the past two days, we've been circulating petitions to all the homerooms for all three grades." She held up a stack of papers. "I have here 253 names of people who support coed football."

The gasp that came from the audience was truly gratifying.

"Now," Lydia said, "we welcome comments and questions."

A teacher got up. "I showed this issue of the *Alternative* to my wife, who is a lawyer. And she said that legally, these students make an excellent case."

Coach Benson looked skeptical. "Are you saying they could sue the school?"

The teacher shrugged. "It's been done before. And successfully."

"Girls can't play football," Coach Benson stated flatly, shaking his head.

"Why not?" Lydia asked.

The coach seemed to be at a loss for words. Finally, he just barked, "Because they don't have the guts!"

Sam Kelsey rose and spoke over his shoulder. "I'm sorry to disagree with you, Coach," he said slowly, "but I don't think that's true." He turned to look directly at Lydia. "I know girls who are gutsier than most boys."

Lydia tried to keep a smile from creeping across her face. She didn't succeed.

A tall, athletic-looking girl stood up, her eyes flashing angrily. "Schools spend a lot of money on boys' teams, and hardly anything on girls'. I'm on the girls' basketball team, and we have to buy our own uniforms. The boys' team gets theirs free!"

"What does that have to do with girls playing football?" someone called out.

The girl threw her hands up in frustration. "If the school won't spend money on *our* teams, then they should let us play on the teams that *do* get the money!"

From various parts of the room, pockets of applause erupted. After that, it was a free-for-all. One after another, kids got up and offered support, coming up with reasons Lydia hadn't even thought of. There were objections, too, but not nearly as many as she had expected. Zack Snyder got up every now and then and yelled "This is a joke," but no one paid much attention to him.

When the mayor rose, the room got quiet.

"I'm finding this all quite interesting. It makes me very happy to see our young people concerned about such important issues. Some of you may see this as a joke—" she paused and looked sternly at Zack, who actually seemed to shrivel in his seat, "—but this proposition has significant implications. There may be valid reasons to deny girls the right to play football, but I haven't heard any here. If Cedar Park Junior High chooses to implement a new policy regarding football, you have my support."

Lydia couldn't resist—she automatically started clapping. Martha Jane, Kevin, and Emma joined her, and within seconds practically the whole room was applauding.

As the applause died, George Philips rose to his feet. "I would like to say that the *Cedar Century* will also support the plan for coed football," he said importantly. He paused, as if expecting another round of applause. When it didn't come, his chubby face went red and he sat back down.

And then Mr. Fletcher got up, looking more than a little flustered. "I, uh, had no idea this was such a popular issue," he began.

Lydia could sympathize with him—neither had she!

"But the students have certainly presented their case well," he went on. "I must say I have some reservations. However, I'm not the final authority. Since there seems to be so much support for the idea, I will recommend to the Board of Education that our policy on football team selection be studied and serious consideration given to allowing girls to compete for places on the team."

Again, there was applause, and cheers went up from the *Alternative* staff. A few people in the audience were cheering, too. One of them was Sam.

"Thank you, Mr. Fletcher," Lydia said happily. "I guess the meeting is adjourned. Thanks for coming, everyone."

Still chatting excitedly among themselves, the crowd began to disperse. Lydia felt frozen, unwilling to move and upset the glow that was washing over her.

"We did it!" Martha Jane squealed. She threw her arms around Lydia. Suddenly, they were all hugging each other. Joshua came over to their table, and the pride in his eyes when he looked at Emma was unmistakable.

Daphne, Cassie, and Phoebe came running up to Lydia. "Congratulations!" they chorused. Even Cassie looked proud of her. And Daphne didn't look the least bit upset.

"Congratulations," came another voice, a masculine one. Sam had approval written all over his face.

"You surprised me," Lydia said. "I didn't think you'd be in favor of this. Why didn't you tell me?"

"How could I tell you!" Sam exclaimed. "You never let me get a word in! You know, Lydia, maybe if you just listened once in a while instead of running your mouth nonstop, you'd find out you have more friends than you think!"

Lydia's mouth fell open. For once in her life, she was at a total loss for words.

Sam took advantage of the situation. "You didn't even give people a chance to *think* about this idea of yours. Just because they didn't jump to follow you doesn't mean they're all jerks. Some people just aren't as quick to take a stand."

Lydia stared at him. Something about what he'd just said . . . where had she heard it before? And then it came to her.

"It was you! You're the one who sent me that anonymous letter!"

Sam's face turned pink. And then he nodded. "Yeah. I thought you could use some encouragement."

Lydia couldn't speak. How many more surprises did this day have in store for her? As it turned out, there was yet another to come.

Sam moved closer to her. "Look, I was wondering . . . would you like to go to a movie this weekend? Like, maybe Sunday afternoon?"

"A movie? With you?"

Sam laughed. "No, with my grandfather. Hey, didn't we already have this conversation?"

Lydia remembered their talk on the phone, when he'd asked her to the dance, and her face got hot.

"Listen," Sam said in a different tone, "you don't have to if you don't want to. I mean, just because I wrote that letter doesn't mean you owe me anything. I'll still support you, even if you won't go out with me." He paused. "But I wish you would."

Lydia realized that Cassie was still standing there, listening to every word with unconcealed delight. "Yeah, okay, I'll go out with you," Lydia said hastily.

"Congratulations, sweetie!" Mrs. Gray threw her arms around Lydia and gave her a squeeze. "I'm so proud of you! The mayor had to leave, but she told me to tell all of you that she admires your initiative."

Phoebe was hopping up and down. "I knew you could do it! I knew you could do it!"

"You looked so important up there," Daphne added. "It was like watching the president or something."

"And you didn't do anything to embarrass us," Cassie said contentedly.

"Hey, guys, it wasn't just me," Lydia interjected. "I was ready to give up!" She indicated the other kids. "These are the ones who kept the ball rolling."

"But it was *your* idea," Emma said generously.

"Well, I think you all deserve a celebration," Mrs.

Gray said. "How about everyone coming back to our house for pizza?"

"Sounds good to me!" Kevin said.

"Uh, Mrs. Gray, can Joshua come, too?" Emma asked.

"Sure," Mrs. Gray said. "The more the merrier."

Lydia turned to Sam. Suddenly she felt oddly shy. "Sam, would you like to come, too?"

"I thought you'd never ask."

They all started to troop out of the school. Cassie clutched Lydia's arm.

"Have you felt the tingle yet?" she asked mischievously, her eyes straying to Sam.

"Sure," Lydia said.

Cassie nodded complacently, and Lydia grinned.

"I always get a tingle when I win!"

12

L YDIA'S GOT A BOYFRIEND," Phoebe sang out.

"Shut up," Lydia said good-naturedly as she took her seat at the table. "Pass the eggs, please."

"Actually, I think Fee has a point," Mr. Gray mused. "Let's see, that fellow—what's his name again?"

"Sam," Lydia replied as she reached for the juice.

"Ah yes, Sam. Now, he was here Thursday evening for dinner, right? And as I recall, there were a couple of phone calls on Friday and Saturday. And if my memory serves me right, he came for you yesterday—"

"—and we went to the movies," Lydia finished. Her father's teasing wasn't bothering her one little bit. "Okay, what's your point?"

"I'm just puzzled, that's all. Here it is, Monday morning, we've all been up for at least an hour, and I haven't seen or heard from the young man. Amazing."

Daphne giggled. "Lydia was so mean to him all last week. And Sam wouldn't give up! I think that's amazing."

"What's really amazing," Cassie broke in, "is that here's Lydia, who doesn't even *try* to flirt and who doesn't dress right and who doesn't do anything with her hair—but who's got a boyfriend! Not just an ordinary boyfriend, either—a football player! And he's cute!" She sighed mournfully. "It's totally unbelievable."

"I wouldn't say that," Mr. Gray objected. "Maybe, unlike your typical adolescent male, this Sam has some taste."

"I just hope he has some friends," Cassie said. "This is so depressing. Here Daphne has Rick and Lydia has Sam and I don't have anyone. I'm the only one without a boyfriend."

"*I* don't have a boyfriend," Phoebe reminded her.

"Oh, yeah? What about that funny-looking kid who's always hanging around?"

Phoebe looked mildly offended. "I don't think Leonard's funny looking. And he's not my boyfriend." She cocked her head to one side thoughtfully. "On the other hand, he *is* a boy. And he *is* my friend. So I guess maybe he is my boyfriend. In a way."

"Isn't this nice," Mrs. Gray said, entering the kitchen. "Breakfast on the table and we're all here, eating together."

"Except I've got to go," Cassie said, getting up.

Lydia turned to her in surprise. "*You're* going to school early?"

Cassie nodded. "Gary Stein sometimes gets to homeroom early. It's a good opportunity to start working on him again." With a wave, she grabbed her books and jacket from the counter and ran out the back door.

"Boy, it's a good thing I didn't have to work that hard for a boyfriend," Lydia murmured. "Sam and I would never have gotten together."

"The Board of Education is meeting this morning," Mrs. Gray commented as she helped herself to breakfast. "I wonder if they'll be acting on the football recommendation."

"Are you nervous?" Daphne asked Lydia.

Lydia thought about it. Strangely enough, she couldn't actually say she felt nervous at all. "Not really," she said. "It's funny. Once I knew we had the support of the kids at school, I felt like we'd won the battle."

The doorbell rang. "I'll get it," Lydia said. She left the kitchen and went to the front door. Sam was standing on the doorstep.

"What are you doing here?" Lydia asked in surprise.

Sam grinned. "I thought maybe I could walk you to school."

Lydia raised her eyebrows. "*Walk* me? I'm perfectly capable of walking myself, without assistance."

"Okay, walk *with* you. Better?"

Lydia rewarded him with a big smile. "*Much* better. C'mon in."

"You said you had an *Alternative* meeting this morning," Sam said as he followed her in. "And I was thinking—maybe I could join the staff."

"Really? That's great!"

"The way I figure," Sam continued, "if I join the staff, I'll get to see you more."

Lydia stopped and looked at him severely. "Is that the only reason you're joining?"

"Oh, no!" Sam said hastily. "Honest! I want to work! Hey, give a guy a break, would you?"

Lydia examined him carefully for a moment before relenting. He was probably being honest. And even if he wasn't, well, it *was* flattering.

"Sam's here to walk with me to school," she announced in the kitchen, carefully emphasizing the "with." "And he's going to join the *Alternative* staff."

"What's your next issue about?" Mr. Gray asked.

"We haven't absolutely decided yet," Lydia replied. "But we're thinking about campaigning for a Teacher of the Year Award."

"Now that's what I call an excellent idea," Mrs. Gray remarked. "We teachers don't get the recognition we deserve."

"I guess," Lydia said. "Mainly, we think it might give them the incentive to improve their performance."

Mrs. Gray's eyes turned heavenward. "Gosh, that's awfully nice of you."

"See ya," Sam said as he and Lydia walked out the back door.

"No doubt about that," Mr. Gray called after them.

"Today's meeting," Lydia told Sam, "is mostly going to be about money. We plan to get the school to

125

acknowledge us as an official organization so we can apply for funding. Then we can print the *Alternative* like a real newspaper."

"Lydia, you're really something," Sam said, "even if you do have a big mouth."

Lydia opened it to respond, and then clamped it shut. Might as well let him finish.

"You know," Sam went on, "I could see you becoming the first woman president of the United States."

Lydia nodded in agreement. Then her brow wrinkled. "But I won't be eligible to run for twenty-one years. I'm assuming they'll elect one before *that*."

It was during third period that Lydia heard her name over the loudspeaker, along with Kevin's and Martha Jane's and Emma's. They were being summoned to the principal's office, and Lydia had a pretty good idea what for.

They all arrived at the same time, and the secretary ushered them into Mr. Fletcher's office.

"I just had a call from the Board of Education," the principal said.

Lydia could tell from his expression that the news wasn't what they'd hoped to hear. "Did they turn down the recommendation?"

"Not exactly," Mr. Fletcher said. "They said the situation will be reviewed and explored and studied."

"In other words," Kevin remarked, "they're giving us the runaround."

"I wouldn't say that," Mr. Fletcher began, and then

he grinned. "But I wouldn't say you're absolutely wrong in your assessment."

"What can we do about it?" Emma asked.

"Not much, I'm afraid. My guess is that they just see football as such a physically demanding sport, they're reluctant to jump into a coed program. But don't be too disappointed. At least they've agreed to look into the possibilities. Of course, that will take some time. . . ."

"A *long* time," Lydia noted.

"True," Mr. Fletcher said. "But you can't change the world overnight."

"I know," Lydia sighed. "It takes at least a few weeks."

Mr. Fletcher rose, indicating that the meeting was over. "Keep up the good work, kids. I'm looking forward to the next issue of the *Alternative*."

Lydia exchanged glances with the others. "About the *Alternative*, Mr. Fletcher," she said. "We want to become an official student organization so we can get some money."

Mr. Fletcher held up a hand. "That's a Student Council decision, Lydia, you know that."

Lydia grinned. "We just thought it might help our case if we had your support."

"I'll give it serious consideration," Mr. Fletcher said, going to the door and holding it open for them.

Martha Jane grimaced. "You mean, you'll review it and study it and explore it—"

"—and I'll get back to you next week," Mr. Fletcher promised.

Back in the outer office, Martha Jane shook her head sadly. "Well, I guess we gave it our best shot."

"And we can't win them all," Emma added.

"Yeah," Lydia said. "And at least we got kids thinking about some important things."

"That's right," Kevin said. "On to the next issue! I'll see you guys later."

Lydia went out to the hall and found Sam there waiting for her.

"I was in Kevin's class when you guys got called to the office. What happened?"

Lydia told him, and Sam was appropriately sympathetic. They walked together down the hall in silence for a moment.

"You know," Sam said suddenly, "spring isn't all that far off."

"What do you mean?"

"Spring! Baseball! It's not as grueling as football, and there are already girls' softball teams. We could start a campaign for a coed baseball team!"

Lydia thought about it. Interesting idea . . . and they'd already laid the groundwork with their football campaign.

"What do you think?" Sam put his hand on her shoulder.

A familiar tingle went through her. But how familiar was it? Was it coming from Sam's idea? Or . . . was it coming from Sam?

"I'm thinking," Lydia said slowly, "that maybe Cassie isn't so dumb after all."

Sam looked totally confused. "What does that have to do with baseball?"

Lydia laughed. "Nothing. It's a good idea! We'll talk about it with the others."

After all, she decided, she didn't really care if the tingle came from Sam or from Sam's idea. She was perfectly willing to enjoy them both.

Some more titles in Lions Tracks:

Some more titles in Lions Tracks:

☐ **Catch You On the Flipside** *Pete Johnson* £1.95
☐ **The Chocolate War** *Robert Cormier* £2.25
☐ **Rumble Fish** *S E Hinton* £1.95
☐ **Tex** *S E Hinton* £1.95
☐ **Breaking Up** *Frank Willmott* £1.95

All these books are available at your local bookshop or newsagent, or to order direct from the publishers, just tick the titles you want and fill in the form below.

NAME (Block letters) _____

ADDRESS _____

_____

Send to: Collins Childrens Cash Sales, PO Box 11, Falmouth, Cornwall, TR10 9EP

I enclose a cheque or postal order or debit my Visa/Mastercard to the value of the cover price plus:

UK: 60p for the first book, 25p for the second book, plus 15p per copy for each additional book ordered to a maximum charge of £1.90.

BFPO: 60p for the first book, 25p for the second book plus 15p per copy for the next 7 books, thereafter 9p per book

Overseas and Eire: £1.25 for the first book, 75p for the second book, thereafter 28p per book.

Credit card no: _____

Expiry Date: _____

Signature: _____

Lions reserve the right to show new retail prices on covers which may differ from those previously advertised in the text or elsewhere.

Some more titles in Lions Tracks:

- ☐ **Slambash Wangs of a Compo Gormer**
  Robert Leeson £2.50
- ☐ **The Bumblebee Flies Anyway** *Robert Cormier* £1.95
- ☐ **After the First Death** *Robert Cormier* £2.25
- ☐ **That Was Then, This Is Now** *S E Hinton* £1.95
- ☐ **Centre Line** *Joyce Sweeney* £2.25

Some more titles in Lions Tracks: